HANDLE WITH CARE

HANDLE WITH CARE

AND OTHER STORIES

Ann MacLaren

Matador
9 Priory Business Park,
Wistow Road, Kibworth Beauchamp,
Leicestershire. LE8 0RX
Tel: 0116 279 2299
Email: books@troubador.co.uk
Web: www.troubador.co.uk/matador
Twitter: @matadorbooks

ISBN 978 1789016 062

British Library Cataloguing in Publication Data.
A catalogue record for this book is available from the British Library.

Printed and bound by CPI Group (UK) Ltd, Croydon, CR0 4YY
Typeset in 11pt Baskerville by Troubador Publishing Ltd, Leicester, UK

Matador is an imprint of Troubador Publishing Ltd

For Iain

Contents

Acknowledgements

My thanks to Mary Edward for proofreading this work, to Kirsty MacLaren for her artwork, to the team at Matador for their help and guidance through all stages of the publication process, and to Strathkelvin Writers' Group for their support and encouragement.

Burnt Umber

Mariella was a worrier. She was the sort of woman who never went to the toilet on a train because she worried that the automatic door would automatically open and she'd be caught with her knickers down. The sort who always turned up early – in case she was late.

Mostly, she worried that the worst might happen – and not for nothing, she would point out, because very often the worst did indeed happen: she *had* failed the exams that would have taken her to University, she *hadn't* managed to get pregnant, her husband *had* become tired of her and left her for a younger model, she *had* ended up an unhappy and lonely old woman.

Mariella was actually only forty five, but she considered herself old. And while she may have felt lonely at times she wasn't always alone: she very often had a man about the house – although it's true to say that none of these men ever made her happy. Because Mariella was drawn to an unsuitable man like a wasp to a rotten apple. And this was something else she worried about.

There was Tony, who was always borrowing money but never paid it back; Ken, whose wife didn't understand him; and Rick, who came from Alabama on business trips and used her home like a hotel. None of the three was a serious contender for a long-term relationship.

Her friend Connie took her to task about this:
"Why do you let yourself be so put upon? Get shot of the lot of them and see if you can't find yourself a decent man, somebody who can take care of you and not lean on you the way they all do. There's lots of men out there, you just have to know where to look. What about a dating website?"

Connie could fit more words into ten seconds than anyone else she knew.

"I've tried a dating website. I didn't like it."

"You didn't like it because you weren't prepared to give it a proper go, 'cos when you were sent those four names and four photos, you didn't believe what you saw in front of your nose. You were convinced they'd be con men or mass murderers."

It was true. But she'd felt she had reason to be sceptical. Each reply was computer generated; there was nobody there, no real person inside that screen smiling out at her, making her feel safe and secure. Mariella didn't trust computers.

Connie rattled on like a train.

"Join a club then, that's a great way of meeting people, a walking club maybe. Or volunteer in a charity shop, they're crying out for help. Or get a part-time job, in a café. No, wait, I've got a great idea, what about a night class? A lot of men go to classes and they'll at least have a modicum of intelligence. What would you like to learn, a language? Spanish? Greek? Or what about Art, you were always good at that at school. You might do Life Drawing classes, naked men, just imagine…"

"I don't like walking; you get all sweaty and if it rains it's miserable. And what would be the point of learning a language? I don't go anywhere. You know I'm terrified of flying, and I don't like ferries either. Too much water. And before you say it, I'm not going through that tunnel." Mariella shivered at the thought.

"You're impossible, I'm off home," said an unusually abrupt Connie. And she was gone – which was a pity because she didn't hear Mariella say:

"It's been a long time since I did any painting; I'd probably be rubbish at it, but I'd quite like to give it a try."

Mariella had liked painting as a child; but more than that, she'd loved the accessories that went with it. In her bedroom she'd had a deep drawer full of various colouring books and pads of paper, all neatly stacked to one side in their different sizes. At the other side her large crayon collection was kept, separated by colour, in cigar boxes, which she would check regularly in case her brother had been borrowing them and a red had become mixed up with the greens. She'd even had a few pieces of charcoal wrapped in paper and hidden at the back of the drawer, but she hadn't used these much because they were a bit messy. On top of the boxes sat her prized possession: a tin of watercolours handed down from an aunt, with scenes from Alice in Wonderland on the top and inside a selection of named rectangles of colour. It had never been used, and Mariella hadn't wanted to spoil it by using it either, but she had spent hours just looking at it, learning and falling in love with the names of the colours – Prussian blue, ultramarine, vermilion, yellow ochre, and her most favourite, burnt umber. She would roll the name around her tongue and think of her mother's ginger cake.

Connie was right: at school Mariella had been good at drawing and painting. One of her teachers had suggested to her that she might want to try for Glasgow School of Art, but she wasn't sure she'd like living there. She'd heard stories. Anyway, her mother had other ideas.

"You don't want to waste your time on all that arty-farty stuff, Mariella. It's not a real career. You want to be a doctor, or a lawyer – something that'll make you a bit of money."

Later, when it was clear Mariella was lacking in the academic department, her mother had other suggestions.

"You could be a hairdresser, that's a bit of an art, isn't it?"

Mariella had felt sick at the thought of having to wash greasy heads, and pull swirls of hair out of plug holes. Eventually she found an easy and undemanding job as receptionist in an insurance office.

When Connie phoned to apologise for her rapid exit the night before, Mariella had news for her.

"I've decided to sign up for an Art class. A beginner's class, I don't want anything too difficult. I'll send away for a brochure and see what the university has to offer."

"You don't want to bother with all that palaver," said Connie, who was clearly sitting in front of her computer because Mariella could hear her tapping at the keyboard. "Here it is, I've got it – Creative Drawing and Painting Beginners, a practical approach to drawing and painting for people with no previous experience. Through a variety of demonstrations and lessons you will develop your practical skills, using a range of materials and different painting techniques. Ten sessions, materials not provided. Tutor, Frankie Amadei, mmm… I like the sound of him, must be Italian. I'll book you onto the course, I'm online anyway. I'll book myself on too, I'm not doing anything else on Thursday evenings."

Mariella had a wonderful dream that night. She was in an Art studio, alone except for a naked model – a man about her own age, bronzed, muscled, stretched out in an artistic pose on a piece of white silk cloth on a raised podium in the centre of the room. Around the studio were an assortment of easels holding large canvases, and on these Mariella had drawn or painted her model, or parts of him, from various angles and in different media. One easel held a pencil drawing of his feet, another a charcoal of his hands, a third a pastel of his head and shoulders, a fourth a study of his back and bottom in oils. They were all perfectly executed. She looked around for the watercolours to begin her final painting, a full frontal view of her model, and found a small box of paints containing rectangles of colour. She dipped her brush in water and began. In a very short time she had completed her work, except for the groin area which she had been avoiding looking at. Now she took a deep breath and stared at the penis for longer than was perhaps necessary; it was quite small, but lay against the white thigh at a jaunty angle. She wondered which colour would portray it most faithfully; but when she turned to survey her box of paints there was only one rectangle left. Burnt umber.

"Unusual, but original," said the tutor-model as he came behind her to survey the finished picture. "I love the burnt umber. Makes it stand out." He held her shoulders in his strong hands and leaned over to whisper in her ear. "It's my favourite colour."

Mariella woke panting and sweating. She lay there, breathless, trying to hold on to the intense pleasure of her dream, but it became fuzzy and began to dissipate along with the details of her art work, the tutor, the naked body.

Room 601 the letter said. Mariella checked it in the lift going up to the sixth floor, then again when she was standing outside the door. The room was in darkness; there was no-one around. Still, it was only 6.45 and the class wasn't due to start till 7.30. Best to be early. People would arrive soon. Mariella waited. And waited.

When nobody had arrived by 7 she began to worry. The tutor ought to have been here by now to set up.

Perhaps the venue had been changed to a different room; she should have checked with the janitor when she came in. She'd better do that now. She wondered if she should walk down the stairs, checking the rooms on each floor, but decided that would take too long.

Mariella stepped back into the lift and pressed the button for the ground floor. The door started to close, stalled, opened again then closed properly, and in those few seconds she heard the lift beside hers open its doors, spilling out a chattering of voices and laughter. She was sure she could hear Connie's silly high-pitched giggle in there somewhere.

"Damn" she said loudly and pressed the floor 6 button. Too late. The lift didn't stop. She pressed 5, 4, 3, 2, and 1, but the lift continued descending. When it reached the ground floor it stopped, but the doors didn't open. Mariella pressed 6 again and the lift began to move up through all the floors, stopping at 5. The doors stayed shut. Exasperated, she pressed 6 again, but the lift began to descend. She jabbed at all the numbers again in quick succession, including the Open and Close buttons. The lift slowed, then jerked to a halt. The doors remained closed. There was no number on the display. Anxiously she hit the doors open button again. Nothing.

Mariella was very worried. She punched the alarm button, expecting to hear a siren and reassuring voices outside the lift; but there was only silence. In a panic she hit it again, and again, and again… till suddenly a crackly voice emerged from the speaker:

"Okay, okay, keep your hair on. I was in the loo. When a man's gotta go, he's gotta…"

"I'm stuck in a lift," shouted Mariella.

"Yes, I know that. Obviously."

"Just get me out of here. Please!"

"Just calm yourself down, Missus. Take big deep breaths. I'll get somebody to you as soon as I can. Could you just give me the long number that's up at the top of the control panel. I need to cross reference. Take your time now, we want to get it right."

"Never mind the bloody number! Just get me out of here. I'm in the first lift just past your office…"

"Eh, no. My office doesn't have a lift. And you're in a building in… let's see… Edinburgh. At least, that's what it says on the screen here. I'm in an industrial estate just outside Dundee."

"Are you not the janitor? Where's the janitor? Can he not open the door? Pleeeease!"

"Doesn't have the wherewithal," the voice said. "But don't you worry, I've got a man on his way. Just you give me that number so that I can do my cross check, then you can relax. We'll have you out of there in no time."

Mariella looked for the number.

"It's 32675," she said, in a shaky voice.

"No, that can't be it. It should have six digits. And there should be two letters in front of it. Are you looking in the right place?"

"I'm looking at the control panel!" She shouted. "It's right there at the top! Above all the numbers!"

"No, no, not that control panel. The one up high that controls the electrics."

Mariella stood on tiptoe and tried to read the number.

"It's too high," she wailed.

"Try jumping up to them. You can give me the numbers one at a time, that's only eight jumps."

Mariella started to bounce. The floor shook worryingly, but she persevered.

"G… G… 2… 1… 4… 4… 1… 2."

"Great. You sound a bit out of puff. Why don't you sit down and have a wee rest, get your breath back. The engineer'll be there in a jiffy. Will we sing something to pass the time? Do you like Abba?"

They were on *Dancing Queen* when the engineer prised open the doors between the ground and basement. A small crowd of men and women – headed by Connie and her new friend Tutor Frankie, who looked about as Italian as a haggis supper – watched the operation, giving advice and assistance. The janitor managed to lower down a chair for her to stand on, and the men pulled her to safety. Not that she had been in any real danger, they told her.

Mariella wasn't convinced. She could – as Connie was now busy telling her – have run out of air in that confined space, or had a heart attack. She'd never thought she'd be so pleased to hear Connie's voice.

"Oh look, Frankie, she's shaking. Let's take her down to the pub for a drink. I'd need a drink if I'd been stuck in the lift. And look at your tights Mariella, they're all ripped. They could have been more careful pulling you out. Lucky for you Frankie's cancelled the class. No heating. He says it wouldn't be fair on the model."

The large glass of wine calmed her a bit, but she refused a second; she didn't want to play gooseberry for the rest of the evening. She headed home to a warm bath and a worry.

Mariella had just tucked herself into bed when her mobile rang. It would be Ken needing to talk, she thought, as she felt for the phone on her bedside table, or Tony looking for a loan, or Rick, off a late flight and wanting a warm bed. Or even, she decided, as she hurled the phone across the room, a gloating Connie. When it stopped ringing she settled herself under the covers again, took some deep calming breaths, and conjured up – as she had done every night since that heavenly dream – the vision of a bronzed, young man against a white silk background; she remembered the clasped hands, the curve of his feet, the ripple of his white thigh, and she began to relax into the now familiar feelings of peace, happiness and exquisite pleasure.

Mariella drifted off to sleep, her mind focused on burnt umber.

Pat the Pig

Trish gave the soft doughy roll an affectionate squeeze as she sliced through it with the bread knife, then she placed four thick slices of Mars Bar on top of one half, covered the other half with chocolate spread, joined the two, and with a sigh of contentment sank her teeth into it.

The diet was broken. She knew that shame and remorse lay not very far ahead, but what the hell, she might as well enjoy the moment. So she managed to savour every mouthful of the roll, polish off the leftovers of the Mars Bar and lick the chocolate-smeared knife before the pangs of guilt crept up on her.

Hunger pangs and no guilt or guilt pangs and no hunger, thought Trish. I can't win.

She had always been overweight. Fat Pat, she had been called on her first day at school. And the name, like the fat, had stuck. She was still Fat Pat when she left twelve years later. There were other names too – Blob, Blubber, Hippo – the usual stuff, but only one other school nickname had lasted any length of time. That had been because of an altercation with one of the nuns at the dinner table one day, a particularly malicious nun who had seen Trish helping herself to seconds.

"Gluttony is a sin, Patricia," she had announced to the whole dining hall. "Think of the starving children in Africa."

Trish should have kept her mouth shut. But the opportunity to draw attention to the nun's faulty logic was too good to miss.

"Is it not a worse sin to waste the food, Sister? All these leftovers just go to the pigs."

"And isn't that why you're eating them?" said the nun, smiling around the room to give the other girls permission to appreciate the joke. Which they did. Loudly.

"Pat the pig!" someone squealed, pointing at the bright pink Trish, and some of the girls at her table stretched out their hands, laughing, to give her a pat on the head. The name had stuck for months, the gesture even longer.

As soon as she left school she began calling herself "Trish".

❧

The Mars Bar roll had whetted her appetite. Trish peeked out from behind the kitchen door to see if the coast was clear, took two large steps towards the front hall, and grabbing her jacket with one hand and the doorknob with the other took a deep breath and shouted towards the living room.

"I'm just off out to post a letter!"

She was downstairs and out in the street before the door banged shut. No chance for Josie to catch her. Her sister would know she was lying, know she was making a beeline for the chippy and the welcoming, hot embrace of a pie supper or some such forbidden pleasure. But Josie wouldn't follow her, wouldn't want to embarrass herself by remonstrating with her in public, telling her to exercise some self-control, to stop gorging herself on that fried muck, and if she didn't lose some of the layers of flab hanging around her body she'd never get any man to look at her twice.

Trish hurried down the road and out of sight of the house, sweat beginning to prickle at every fold of her skin. As she rounded the corner she could see that there was no-one at the bus stop, which was unfortunate, because there was a bus stopped at the lights behind her, and she'd have to sprint if she wanted to catch it. Well, not a sprint actually, more of a fast wobble. She wondered if she should let the bus go, and walk to the chippy, use up some of the calories from the Mars Bar roll. Everybody said you'd be quicker walking to the shops because there were so many sets of traffic lights in the area. But it was quite a distance, and anyway, running for the bus would use up the same amount of calories, wouldn't it? She hurried forward and got to the bus stop in time, although she slipped, exhausted, as she was getting on and ended up on one knee in front of the driver, who had to come out of his cab to help her up and into a seat. That'll have given the other passengers their money's worth, Trish thought. Nothing like seeing somebody else coming to grief to give you a good laugh. Just like that programme on the telly with the video clips of people crashing their bikes into telegraph poles or falling off swings or cracking their heads on tables when they fall while they're dancing at some wedding. Hilarious.

It was at least five minutes before she got her breath back properly, and more before the feeling of nausea that she always got after any physical activity left her. The bus was filling up, mostly young people going to the pub or the pictures, and women heading for a night at the Bingo. An old man got on and stopped beside Trish's seat, looking down at the enormous thighs taking up the space of two people and waiting for her to somehow magically reduce her bulk so that he could squeeze in beside her. She ignored him.

"It's no' healthy that," he said in a loud murmur as he staggered towards a seat further back. Trish stayed calm.

"You wouldn't say that to an anorexic," she called back to him for the rest of the bus to hear, "and that's not healthy either."

"You tell 'im hen," one of the Bingo women backed her up, and another added "Cheeky auld bugger."

"At least he only takes up wan seat," shouted a young boy who was sitting opposite Trish, grinning arrogantly, arm wrapped round a delicate young set of bones covered in skin. But as the target of his remark stood up his smile faded and he clutched his girlfriend protectively, thinking that maybe he should have kept his stupid mouth shut like the woman behind him was suggesting. Trish, who had only stood up because the bus had reached her stop, laughed at his obvious assumption and nodding towards him announced to the bus in general, "Big man, eh?" They were all laughing as she got off the bus, triumphant. Just as well Josie wasn't there. Josie would have been not just plain old embarrassed. She would have been mortified.

Trish wondered, as she often did, what life would be like if she was slim and attractive like Josie. Imagine. To be able to walk into a shop and ask for a size ten skirt, or a pair of skin-tight trousers. To be able to get a job in an office where you have to power dress, and have the boss asking for you to be his PA. To be able to go clubbing and have your pick of men wishing they had the nerve to speak to you, to ask you out, to get you into bed as soon as possible. Like Josie. Trish wished she had a boyfriend to get into bed with. She thought about sex quite a lot.

Right now though, the hot satisfying pleasure she was looking for had a definite calorific slant.

"Gluttony is a sin, Patricia."

That day at school the nun's voice had crept into her brain and taken up permanent residence. She heard it at every meal, every mouthful. But she couldn't bear the thought of a life without real food. The kind of food that fills your stomach, that radiates warmth and comfort to the very tips of your fingers and toes. Gravy and mashed potatoes, pie and chips, syrup sponge and custard. Was that gluttony? How could enjoying your food be a sin? She wasn't taking it out of someone else's mouth.

She imagined the menus of a perfect day. Sausages, bacon and eggs for breakfast with a mountain of hot buttered toast. A mid-morning cappuccino with a chocolate croissant. Thick creamy soup followed by a couple of cheese rolls for lunch. Afternoon tea with scones, jam and cream. Stew and dumplings with peas and mash then apple crumble and custard for dinner. Heaven.

No need to sneak out for a furtive fish supper after that lot, thought Trish.

Food. She got hungry just thinking about it. As she headed up the road towards the chip shop she wondered what she should treat herself to. She didn't feel the need for this in-between feed every night. Often she could make do with a couple of bags of crisps or a bar of chocolate. It just depended on how much she had been allowed to eat at dinner time, and that depended on her mother's mood. One day she would insist they all ate salads to lend Trish moral support, the next she'd cook macaroni cheese and chips, telling Trish that she had only to eat smaller portions. She didn't know which was worse – a large helping of rabbit food or a tiny portion of something delicious that made her ache for more. The best days were when her mother decided that diets didn't work and everybody should just eat what they liked because life was short and there was no point in being miserable all the time.

Her mother wasn't overweight like Trish, or thin like Josie. She was just normal. About a size sixteen. She wouldn't mind settling for being the same size as her mother. Ordinary. Not slim, but not fat either. A healthy size sixteen. Maybe that would be easier, thought Trish. More achievable.

She could visualise herself as a size sixteen, see her own face, complete with double chins, on top of this smaller but still rounded body. Whenever she had tried to imagine herself as a size ten it was always Josie's face she saw, not her own. So maybe it was impossible to be like Josie, and if she set herself an impossible target she was bound to fail. Surely she could manage size sixteen.

She stopped, breathless from her physical and mental exertions, opposite the chip shop at the top of the road, and considered the enormity of the challenge.

Well, she would just cut down a bit. Not her mother's cutting down that reduced a meal to snack proportions, but just a little less than what she'd been used to. That's the advice you see in all these slimming books and magazines. A couple of pounds a week, even one pound. Not too fast, because if you starve yourself you'll get hungry and give up, and as soon as you start eating normally the weight will pile on again and you'll be fatter than ever. That's what they say. Trish knew she ate too much but, she reasoned with herself, if she only had to cut down a little she could still eat quite a lot. She wouldn't ever need to feel hungry, wouldn't need to stop eating all her favourite foods. She would take it slowly. Very, very slowly. One day at a time. Or one week at a time. She would give herself a target of one year. And she would aim at a pound a week. Hardly anything at all. But a pound a week, for a year, that's fifty two pounds. Three stone ten pounds. Say three and a half to allow for any hiccups. That would take her down to at least a size eighteen, not much bigger than her mother. A pound a week would be easy, surely. She might even try to walk a bit more often or buy an exercise video, then maybe she'd lose two pounds some weeks.

Confidently, resolutely, she crossed the road and pushed open the door of the chip shop, into the smell of deep frying and the crackling of hot fat. As she moved slowly forward in the queue, past the golden array of crispy, battered food, past the mound of succulent chips glistening behind the glass counter, she closed her eyes and inhaled deeply.

Slowly, she repeated to herself. One day at a time. It would be difficult. So difficult. But she would try to be strong.

"A pie and a sausage," she announced as she reached the head of the queue, and added quietly. "And a portion of chips."

Tomorrow. She'd start the diet tomorrow.

Handle With Care

As she sat at the window watching, waiting for the baby to arrive, Rose felt as if she was in labour, but without the pains. Excited, worried, wondering if it would all turn out okay – all the emotions she'd felt thirty years ago, as an eighteen-year-old about to become a single mother. She'd coped better than anyone had given her credit for, brought Paul up without the help of family and the support of only a few friends. It had been a struggle; but this would be child's play in comparison. She smiled at the unintended pun.

She wondered vaguely what Paul would say, but she didn't really care. They had always been so close, but when he met Anna that had changed. Once they were married he had moved away, physically and emotionally.

She had hoped grandchildren would bring them close again, but when Louise was born she had been allowed to hold her for only a few short minutes before Anna's mother had arrived to gather up the baby, hand out advice and organise the family. It was clear that it was Anna's mother who would take precedence, would help out, do the babysitting. Would be the proper grandmother. Paul wouldn't argue; anything for a quiet life. What was it her own grandmother used to say? A son's a son till he takes a wife... Rose didn't have any daughters to compensate.

Then one day, when Louise was three months old, Paul had phoned her.

"We wondered if you'd like to babysit. On Saturday night, just for a couple of hours. We've got tickets for a show and Laura's mother's got flu, so we're stuck. I'll come and pick you up."

He didn't even have the tact to lie. She was second choice. She swallowed her pride and said yes, because there was nothing she wanted more than to spend time with Louise. And in spite of Anna's warnings not to lift her, she had picked the baby up from her cot and cuddled her till her arms ached. Rose didn't regret it, even though her arms ached still. But now it was from absence.

As the months passed, the more she thought about her granddaughter the more she missed her. She found herself going for a walk in the park on her days off just so that she could see the mothers, fathers or grannies pushing prams. She'd swallow her jealousy, smile at their babies, ask their names, chat for a while. People were always delighted if you stopped to admire their baby; it was all very sociable. She wished she could have Louise in her pram to wheel along so that people would stop and speak to her. They'd marvel at her baby's beautiful rosy cheeks and shock of black hair, and she would tell them, yes, she looks just like her Daddy did at that age. Oh, she desperately wanted to have a baby in her arms again. She was too old, of course; well past the menopause. But there were other solutions. She decided to speak to Milla.

Milla was a therapist in the nursing home where Rose worked. She was from Romania. She only worked part-time at the home; another part of her time was spent on what she called her 'baby business'. Milla was kind and sympathetic. Rose explained about her granddaughter, about how excluded she felt, and lonely. Very lonely.

"I think you'd be the ideal candidate," said Milla after she had explained all the ins and outs. "Have a think about it for a couple of weeks. I know it's a lot of money. I've got a DVD you can watch."

She'd thought about it and decided yes. She was sure it would be worth it.

Rose was finding it difficult to sit still. She got up to make a third cup of tea but decided to make a sandwich instead. It was too early for lunch, but she had been up since six and hadn't eaten breakfast. It would help the time pass. Watching at the window wouldn't make Ioana arrive any sooner. Ioana. It was a strange name, but she supposed it was the Romanian form of Joanna. She had already decided to change that, but she wanted to wait and see what the baby really looked like. She'd seen photos, of course, but that wasn't the same. She wanted to be sure.

She boiled an egg, cooled it a little under water and began to peel it; it would be too soft to slice but she would mash it up in a cup. That was how Paul had liked his eggs when he was little. He'd sit up tall in his high chair, watching as she prepared it for him, a finger of toast ready in each hand to dip into the mixture. Rose pictured him too sitting up in his pram as she proudly pushed it through the park or to the shops. People stopping to talk. It was a good way to make friends; except that she hadn't made many friends. Or hadn't wanted to. She had no intention of introducing a third party into their domestic equation – friend or lover – who might replace her in her son's affections. Paul was hers, only hers; she was all he needed. Till Anna.

Paul would need her again some day. He would phone when he wanted someone to look after Louise, and she was their last resort. And then she would be able to say honestly and, she hoped, without bitterness:

"Sorry. I have my own baby to look after."

The ringing of the doorbell made her jump. Heart thudding, she took a couple of deep breaths and made herself walk slowly to the door.

The delivery man stood there grinning with a big box in his hands. On the side was written, Fragile – Handle with Care.

"Another one Mrs T. You're very popular. Not so big this time. Want me to put it somewhere for you?"

He took it into the dining room for her and laid it on the table. They had become almost friends, he'd been there so often lately: the crib, the high chair, the changing table, the car seat – he'd brought them all. She usually offered him tea at this point, but today she wanted him to leave. Quickly. She fished in her purse for a ten pound note.

"Have a drink on me, Andy. You've been such a help."

Rose had the box opened before Andy had reached his van. She lifted out the top packaging, and carefully undid the bubble wrap.

And there she was. Her baby. Her Reborn. Her Louise.

The Reborn babies that Milla used in the nursing home for the dementia patients, to calm them when they were agitated, looked real enough; but they were mere dolls in comparison to this little darling. She could see the difference immediately.

She picked her up gently and examined her all over. Absolutely perfect as Milla had promised, and looking exactly like Louise. Rose had taken lots of photos on her mobile phone the day she had looked after her, so she had sent some to Milla. She got the idea from the DVD she'd been given: a woman whose little grandson had been taken off to New Zealand had asked for her Reborn to be made to look just like him. She got other ideas too for the baby: a heartbeat, a breathing mechanism, open nostrils and ears, heat pads for body warmth, even a little birthmark on her leg like the one Louise had. It all added up, of course – over two thousand pounds when converted from Romanian leu – but she could see the money had been well spent.

The egg congealed in its cup while Rose sat for most of the afternoon cuddling the baby in her arms, talking softly to her. Later she would open the envelope with the Adoption Certificate and find the space for change of name. She wouldn't call her Louise, that wouldn't be right. She'd be Lulu.

Eventually she took Lulu into her newly painted nursery and laid her on the changing mat.

"We'll get you changed and then we'll go for a nice long walk in that lovely pram I bought for you," said Rose.

She dressed her baby in a pretty all-in-one and added a pink woollen jacket with a hood, then settled her into her pram and tucked a blanket around her. On top she laid a quilt edged with broderie anglaise – it was sunny, but still quite cold outside. Lulu looked so sweet propped up on her pillow, her wee rosy cheeks shining and her black hair escaping from her hat.

Rose wondered if people in the park would see the family resemblance.

At the Crossroads

The house had lain empty for years, but it was still standing, could still be lived in if anyone had a mind to do it up. The roof was intact, but there was very little glass in the windows and the frames were collapsing in on themselves. The smaller cottage up the hill wasn't much more than a pile of rubble now, its roof caved in and grass growing from every gap and crevice. But his father's house – his house now – had fought for its life against the wind, the rain and the pigeons, and here it stood at the north corner of three roads that led to the village, the hills and the sea. At the crossroads.

He didn't need to push hard to open the door, the lock had rusted long ago, and he could tell by the cigarette ends and bits of waste strewn across the floor that others had been there recently. The kitchen was empty except for a once cream-coloured stove and a cracked plastic bucket beside the sink. Here and there he could see bits of grey-green linoleum, with its check pattern barely discernible through the dust. Archie stared at it, and saw a small boy kneeling there, manoeuvring his little cars and trucks along the lines, making a garage of one of the bigger squares.

"Have you fed the hens yet? Get on with your chores boy."

The harsh voice made the child start. Archie too straightened his back, standing almost to attention, watching paralysed as his father reached out and whacked the boy with his stick.

The child disappeared. In reality, he had disappeared when his mother died the day of his eighth birthday. As had his father – at least the father he had known.

Archie shrugged at his shoulders, trying to relax them; he had become tense, his jaw was tight. He took a deep breath as he stepped through to the living room, and immediately his nostrils filled with the bitter, sharp smell of damp wood and cloth mixed with mouse droppings and urine.

A filthy armchair, torn and vomiting grey stuffing, sat below the window with a large, heavy table pushed up against it; the table top was littered with bottles and cans, and cigarette ends that had been stubbed out on its surface. And there, behind the door, was the piano – his mother's piano, missing its lid and with the front bashed in, but with its yellow keys still intact. He was so happy to see it that he laughed out loud – splitting the silence, almost frightening himself. It was his piano too; and Inga's. His father had forbidden him to play it, but Inga always found a way.

Inga. She had come to him from the sea, like a mermaid. Actually, she had come on the ferry – but she'd reminded him of a mermaid with her long black hair and her transparent, white skin. She'd taught him his scales. She came to keep house; but when his father was out of the way, in the fields or at the herring, she would take him on picnics, to swim in the sea and to fish off the pier. Inga had made him happy again; till the man his father had become had made Inga flick her tail in disgust and vanish into the ocean. Inga lived in Canada now. She sent him a postcard once.

In the burst armchair Archie saw his father, in his filthy dungarees, unshaven, a glass of whisky in his hand; himself, at the table, filling in his sums.

"Put those bloody books away, the fire's needing stoked."

"But I've to finish this homework or…"

"Don't defy me, boy!"

Up came the stick; but there was Inga now, standing between them till the stick was lowered. And Archie was saved, for a while. But there had been no more housekeepers.

He couldn't remember his father ever calling him anything but boy; if it hadn't been for school he might have forgotten his own name. Archie loved school – when he was allowed to go. All sorts of excuses were used to keep him at his chores, to avoid the need for paid help. To raise an income his father had to work both the land and the sea, since neither the farm nor the boat brought in enough money on its own. He was one of what the famous poet called 'fishermen with ploughs'. It seemed an excessively romantic term for such a callous, brutal man.

Archie walked through to the back room, the bedroom, where his mother had died. He had been told to go in and kiss her goodbye, and he had done it bravely, to please his distraught father who had hugged him then as they both wept. But he had been wrong to expect any further love or affection, any sensitivity from their shared bereavement. It was the last time his father had touched him, except in anger. The drink took over.

He had tried to keep his mother in his heart, but time had erased her – almost. He had forgotten her voice, her laughter; but he had one small photo, of his mother and father on their wedding day, and for many years he kept it in his wallet so that he could take it out, wherever he was in the world, and remember her. And if he closed his eyes he might see her at the piano, her fingers moving swiftly through *The Grand Old Duke of York* or *Scotland the Brave*, while he marched importantly round the room, with his toy sword aloft to keep his troops in line. He had cut his father out of the picture, of course.

Archie went outside and lit a cigarette. Rose didn't like him to smoke indoors. He was going to ask Rose to marry him; a triumph of hope over experience, given that he'd been married and divorced twice already. His psychiatrist had suggested that perhaps he still saw himself as 'boy'; now it was time to become a man.

He leaned against the car and looked out to sea. Inga had once told him he could reach America if he swam in a straight line west. He'd made it to New York by more conventional means, and had stayed. He had become fond of the city. Now nothing bound him to this land of his ancestors, only bitter memories; he'd torn up his roots and planted them elsewhere. America was home now.

Rose was a Brooklyn girl; a dreamer, with a heart as soft as butter. He knew if he brought her here she'd fall in love with these islands; with the acres of sky and the indigo sea, the cliffs filled with puffins and guillemots, the handkerchief fields and the ancient brochs and burial mounds. She'd want to renovate the house, make a garden, grow vegetables and keep chickens. The idea horrified him. Best to keep his Brooklyn Rose where she belonged.

Archie took what he needed from the car and returned to the house. He passed the tiny boxroom that had been his own bedroom, but didn't go in. He saw through the open door the window he'd stood at night after night, looking up the hill towards the empty cottage, hoping and praying that somebody would come and live in it; somebody who'd be his friend. It was the same window he'd climbed out of when he ran away, thirty pounds stolen from his father in his pocket to pay for the ferry to the mainland and the bus south.

Back in the sitting room, Archie opened out the newspapers he'd bought that morning. He scrunched up the pages and stuffed some into the ripped seat of the armchair; he placed the rest inside the piano. He stared at the chair for a short time, wondering if his father would appear, then he struck a match. He hoped it would take first time.

For Better, For Worse

Just a stupid wee fall, but he's broken his hip and for weeks you've had to help him wash and dress and make sure he doesn't walk about without his crutches, and he's bored and bad-tempered so you've been pushing him around the shops and museums in a borrowed wheelchair just to get you both out of the house, and you're exhausted and wish to God one of your big sons would think of coming over to take him out of your hair for a couple of hours or one of their wives would offer to have you over to their place for a meal, but they don't, and you know they never will and they'll find all sorts of excuses if you ask, and you don't know how long you can go on like this. And just when you think it can't get any worse he gets up one morning and his leg's all swollen and hard, so you phone the surgery and they tell you to take him to Casualty, and you sit there for over an hour because there's worse cases than him, and when he's eventually seen by a doctor you're sent somewhere else to sit for an hour to wait for a scan, and after another wait you're told he's got a big blood clot in his leg. So he's given some tablets and an injection into his stomach, he's told to come back in the morning for another one, and he's quite depressed when you get him home so you make him his favourite fish pie but he's feeling sick again, he's always feeling sick these days, and he vomits it up on the bedroom carpet during the night. He won't go out now except if it's to the hospital so he just sits in his chair and worries and you don't like to go out and leave him and a couple of days later what he's worried about happens. He gets a pain in his chest and he's a wee bit breathless so you get him back to Casualty and he's seen right away so you know it's serious, and sure enough, a bit of the blood clot has broken off and got into his lung. So they take him up to a ward and give him an oxygen mask and you sit with him for a while but he doesn't want to talk so you leave him there and tell him you'll be back at visiting time. You know you should go into town for some retail therapy or go and get your hair done or treat yourself to a skinny latte and a blueberry muffin, but you just go home and have a good cry and scrub the kitchen floor, and you make an apple crumble to take to him in case he doesn't like the hospital food. And he looks better when you see him at visiting and the doctors must think he's better because the next day they let him out and he looks quite cheerful till you're helping him into the shower at bedtime and he suddenly starts gasping for breath again and you've to phone for an ambulance and while you're waiting he tries to talk about his will and tells you he's sorry and he loves you and you tell him not to be so daft because you're trying to keep it together because you don't want to think he might be dying and you don't want him to think he's dying. And they keep him in for longer this time and he's kept on oxygen but he doesn't look very well and he's running a temperature so they give him antibiotics and he begins to breathe easier and you do too, and he begins to walk about the ward without his crutches, though it's left him with a terrible limp. Things can only get better you say, but they don't because the blood tests they've been doing in the hospital show there's something wrong and the doctor wants to send him for another scan, a full body one this time because anyway, he shouldn't have broken his hip, a man of his age, so you both wait and worry for a few days but avoid talking about it at visiting time and he gets the scan done the day before he's discharged and you both sit at home waiting and worrying again, scared to go out in case the doctor phones with the result, but it's his secretary that phones and she says the doctor wants to see you both together and she says nine o'clock the next morning, so you both know it's bad news but he doesn't want to talk about it and you're glad because you don't know what to say and when you get to the hospital in the morning and the doctor calls you both in you're not surprised when he says the C word, and it's in his bones and they'll do all they can but when you get back outside you're shaking and you want to scream but you see the tears running down his cheeks and you know you'll have to pull yourself together for his sake but you wonder just how long you'll be able to keep it up and who the hell will be around to catch you when you fall.

Moving On

"I'm thinking of selling the house, George. What do you think?"

Evie paused. She wasn't really expecting an answer, but you never knew. With a damp cloth she carefully ironed a smart seam in each leg of George's brown golfing trousers then folded them over a hanger. She picked a blue shirt out of the small heap, and stretched it out on the ironing board.

"Martin thinks it would be for the best," she continued. "He says it's too much for me. But it's not. Really, it's not. I've always liked cleaning, you know that. It was never a chore to me. Polishing and hoovering, sorry George, vacuuming, I know, I know, Hoover's a trade name. And a quick flick around with the duster is all that's needed most days. I don't use half the rooms now. When did we last have visitors to stay? Must have been when your cousin Helen came over from Canada with her family. Remember? We had such a good time with them. Showing them the city. All our favourite haunts. They hadn't known there was so much to see in Glasgow."

She folded the shirt neatly and started on a pair of pyjama bottoms.

"But I suppose he's right. It's too big this place. I'm rattling around in it. It's been almost a year now, he says. As if I needed reminding."

Evie thought about Martin as she straightened the collar of the pyjama jacket. He had sounded anxious last time he phoned. And a bit distracted. Impatient. She expected it had to do with his new business. He was always starting something new. He'd been in Australia for twelve years and he still hadn't settled properly to anything. Maybe he had money worries again. She should have asked him. He seemed relieved when she agreed about the house.

"You won't regret it, Mother," he had said. "It's time to move on."

Martin always called her "Mother". It sounded respectful, but at the same time unaffectionate. Evie could remember the very first time he had addressed her that way. It was on a visit home from university, and he'd brought a girl with him.

"Mother, this is..."

She couldn't remember the girl's name now, but she did remember being addressed as "Mother". So that was it then. She was no longer his Mummy. Not even his Mum.

She looked at the small bundle of clothes beside her. Just some underpants, and a pair of socks left. She didn't need to iron these. Still... she'd just run over them quickly. While she told George about Martin's new business.

"It's something to do with selling holidays. On the Internet. It's taking up a lot of his time. And money. He didn't say as much, but I gather the money he put into the other venture is all gone. He hasn't had much luck, has he? Still, he tries. What he needs is a wife. Or a partner. I know you don't agree with that sort of thing George, but that's the way it is these days. They don't all want to get married. He's leaving it a bit late though. He'll soon be forty. I was thinking, George, I might send him some money when I sell the house. He'd get it anyway when I die. And there should be plenty left, even after I've bought somewhere else. Oh, I know we've given him lots of help in the past. But it's a sad day when you can't help your only son."

Evie moved the hot iron to the worktop in the utility room, then folded the ironing board and put it back in the cupboard. She smiled up at the shelf where the carved wooden casket sat wedged in at the end of a row of cookery books. George had loved her cooking.

"You were always the one who made the decisions. You would have known what to do, if you hadn't been the first to go." She reached out and patted the base of the box, as if for luck, then said softly,

"We'll talk about it later, George."

She picked up the small pile of newly ironed clothes and headed upstairs, where she carefully scrunched up each item before depositing them one by one in the dirty linen basket.

Ball Bearings

I call it the ball-bearing effect. You know, when you're going down a gravelly slope and your foot slips on some stones, and before you know it you can't stop till you land on your backside. If you're lucky the only damage is wounded pride. Of course, you don't need to be up a hill to find a slippery slope. I slipped, metaphorically speaking, on a chocolate digestive biscuit.

I'm in this walking club and we're split into three groups depending on our fitness level. I'm in the middle group, but I should be in the top. I'm very fit. There are thirteen of us and Rita's the leader. Bit of a bossy boots so she's well suited to the task.

Rita had decided we'd go up Ben Lomond – again. We've been up loads of times, but she's got no imagination.

Eight people had called off; they'd probably decided to do something more interesting. Anyway, we'd arranged to meet at the car park at ten o'clock – it was the middle of summer so we didn't have to start too early – but by half past Rita still hadn't arrived.

We were all having a wee swig of coffee out of our flasks, waiting, when the newest member of the group, Joe, came over and offered me a biscuit. I hadn't taken much notice of him before; he'd only been on one walk with the group and Rita had commandeered him that day, but now that he was standing beside me chatting and offering me a share of his food – well, okay, a biscuit, but it was a chocolate digestive – I could see all his good points close up.

By the way he leaned towards me as he spoke, I got the impression he had taken a fancy to me, which was surprising because an anorak and a beanie hat aren't really a good look, if you ask me. But I was flattered, so when he suggested that I take the initiative and lead the walk up the hill before it got any later, and Rita could catch us up, of course I thought it was a wonderful idea.

Paul, who's a bit of a wimp and obviously scared of Rita, thought we should wait another ten minutes, and Eileen backed him up. I think she fancies him. I agreed on five minutes, just to be nice. When Rita still didn't appear, and I said we should set off, Paul argued that if she arrived after we'd left, Rita wouldn't know which of the two paths up the Ben we'd taken; so I decided he and Eileen could take the tourist path and Joe and myself would take the more scenic Ptarmigan route.

It was a lovely day and the views were out of this world. We took our time, really got to know one another actually, and we took lots of selfies. Just as we neared the brow of the last hill before the top, we could hear this screeching, like a strangled hen, and I knew right away it had to be Rita. She was standing up on top of the triangulation pillar watching for us and started screaming like a banshee the minute she had the tops of our hats in sight.

By the time we reached her she was apoplectic – How dare I take the group up the hill without her, I should never have sent the other two on a different route, if something had happened... She went on and on, from up there on her podium, then the insults began to fly: I was an idiot, I was too full of my own importance, I wasn't fit to be a member of the club... on and on she went.

I didn't bother defending myself. I knew what was really bugging her was that I'd been alone with Joe all that time, and she had designs on him herself. So I put my arm through his and moved forward to where Eileen and Paul were sitting having their sandwiches. This meant passing Rita, up there on her roost, and as we did this her boot came out towards me. I thought she was trying to kick me

– although she said later she was just stepping down from the pillar – so I grabbed her ankle to stop her.

It didn't seem like a hard fall, she wasn't up a great height, but she managed to go down with all her weight on one arm. Did I say Rita's quite a hefty girl?

She got the sympathy vote, of course. We had to call the mountain rescue team and they came and brought her down on a stretcher. A bit over the top if you ask me. It was only a fractured wrist and collar bone. The leader of the team gave me a right ticking off when he heard what had happened. In front of Joe too. I was humiliated. I didn't do it deliberately. I was just defending myself.

We all followed the stretcher down to the loch side where an ambulance was waiting. Nobody spoke to me, not even Joe. Rita was basking in all the attention, obviously. I went and stood on the pier at the car park, trying to look suitably contrite and a wee bit dejected, waiting for Joe to come and put his arm around me and tell me everything would be okay, and maybe suggest a wee drink and a bite to eat once we got back to Glasgow. But no. He did come over, but he started on at me about thoughtlessness and responsibility and impulsiveness, and I just thought, I'll show you impulsiveness.

No, I didn't push him into the loch, although I was definitely tempted. But I thought I'd leave with my dignity intact – the little that was left of my dignity anyhow. I just leaned over and kissed his cheek and left him standing there, looking confused. He'll be sorry, I know he will.

No more walking club for me. I'll be striking out on my own in future, and I'll be treading carefully. Avoiding that ball bearing effect.

And I'll definitely be keeping clear of chocolate digestives.

In Concert

The bean dish was a mistake. In fact, the whole Mexican restaurant experience was a mistake. We should have eaten at home before we left, but Ella wanted to make a night of it and was in that "You never take me anywhere" mode.

"I've heard the food's great, Sammy, and it's just round the corner from the Concert Hall. I'll book us a table."

It was nothing to write home about. Ella had a chicken burrito and I had the chilli con carne – more beans than meat, and it was far too spicy so I had to wash it down with a couple of beers. And the service was very slow; we nearly missed the start of the concert.

We don't particularly like classical music, but Madge next door had given us the tickets as a wee thank you for looking after her dog while she was in the hospital for an operation. Bunion. Funny name for a dog, but he's a friendly wee thing. Well, we couldn't not go. And it was an inoffensive piece – Beethoven's Pastoral. I'd heard bits of that before, on the radio.

The concert started well enough, I was quite enjoying the music, but when we were halfway through the second movement my stomach began to make funny sort of burbling noises; you know, a bit like air in the pipes when you turn on the central heating. I've always been bothered by flatulence. Well, I say bothered, but it's other people it bothers really, not me. Anyway, I was sitting there hoping it wouldn't try to compete with the orchestra when I realised it was moving south a bit. It wasn't long before I felt the twinges of colic nipping at me, which wasn't pleasant; but at least the third movement had started – a lot of these classical pieces have three movements, I don't know how I know that, but I do, I must've read it somewhere – so it wouldn't be long till it was finished and I'd get out of the hall quickly and into the street, where I could let rip without it bothering anybody. Except Ella. She's always giving me grief for doing that but what does she expect me to do? Cork it?

I had a quick glance at the programme and saw to my horror that there were five movements in this symphony. Five! Good grief! Don't get me wrong, it was pleasant enough to listen to; but I was a bit distracted by this point. I was feeling very uncomfortable, wondering if I'd make it to the end of the concert, or if I'd have to incur Ella's wrath by getting up and going out before it finished. The music died away and I tried to relax. Three down, two to go.

The fourth movement had barely started when my bowels began to rumble. I wasn't as worried about this as you might think; I don't know if you're familiar with Beethoven's Pastoral, but the fourth movement's the one with the thunder storm. The approaching thunder certainly covered up the wee noises I was making.

And then I remembered – because, as I said earlier, I've heard bits of this music before – we'd soon be moving into the calm after the storm, and it would get quiet. Very quiet. I panicked. I'd have to get up and get out while the thunderstorm provided cover.

Madge had very thoughtfully got us expensive seats, right down near the front and next to the aisle, but Ella had the end seat. She's a big woman, likes to be able to drape herself a bit; she'd have to shift to let me out. She wouldn't be pleased. No matter, my insides were telling me to make a quick exit.

I nudged Ella, who I think had been dozing – although she would deny that, she always says she's just resting her eyes – because she looked at me quite confused. I motioned with my head for her to move and let me out, but she didn't understand.

"Wind," I mouthed, and made to get up.

Ella looked around her, puzzled, then up to the ceiling. She shrugged her shoulders. She told me later she'd thought maybe somebody had organised a strong wind in the hall to coincide with the storm in the music, make it seem more realistic. Stupid woman.

"Me! Wind!" I tried to whisper but it came out like a hiss.

Ella glowered at me and indicated that I should stay in my seat. She did this by flapping her hand at me: I mean, really! You'd think I was a wee boy.

By this time the storm was reaching its peak, and things were taking a turn for the worse in the trouser department. I had to get out of there. Quickly.

I stood up and tried to squeeze past Ella, but instead of moving her big fat legs to the side she just sat tight. I could see she was mad at me. But the storm on stage was passing, and the orchestra was about to progress quietly into the final movement. It was now or never.

I should have known better. I lifted my leg up high to step over Ella, and involuntarily broke wind. It was quite loud, and I might have got away with it, the audience might have thought it was one of the instruments that had gone off key; but as I pulled my other leg over Ella's knees

I inadvertently let fly another. The orchestra slithered to a stop. I headed towards the door trying to look relaxed and unconcerned – though I knew Ella would be livid.

Did I mention this was a Glasgow audience? No polite turning away and pretending nothing had happened here. No sweeping the embarrassing scene under the carpet. No saving of blushes. The silence was broken before I was halfway up the aisle:

"Was that an attempt at the Trumpet Voluntary?" shouted a man up near the back.

"Trumpet involuntary, more like," somebody replied.

People began to laugh, and before I reached the door they were all chipping in their tuppenceworth.

"Sounded like wood-wind to me."

"Better out than in."

"Wherever you be let your wind blow free."

Even the wee woman that held the door open for me as I rushed past felt moved to comment:

"Ye'll feel the better o' that, son."

I hurried outside and made myself comfortable in the fresh air; then I went and sat in the car.

Ella's huff lasted three days. She told me later, once she was speaking to me again, that it took the orchestra fifteen minutes to compose themselves, but when they did, they started again at the beginning of the last movement, and everybody managed not to laugh – although the big man playing the double bass had a huge grin on his face the whole time, and his shoulders were heaving.

And I know Madge has been told the whole story – the way the two of them burst into that "Let it go, let it go..." song when I'm driving them to the shops. You'd think women didn't pass wind. Just wait till Ella does a wee fluff, as she calls it, in public. That'll be a different story.

Ella says she's never showing her face in that concert hall again; says it'll be all the same crowd that goes and she wouldn't want to be recognised, and anyway, she didn't really think that kind of music was for the likes of us. I don't know what she's talking about – it wasn't that bad.

I'm surprised they haven't called me in for an audition.

Old Annie

It was a polystyrene container full of chips and tomato sauce that changed old Annie's life. She could have stepped over it, of course, ignored it, or kicked it into the side like she usually did with the bits of rubbish that accumulated in the close mouth, because it would be gone anyway in a couple of days. The seagulls would make short work of the chips, the empty container would be picked up by the wind and deposited in the middle of the road where it would be reduced to fragments by a passing car, then dispersed along the length of the street to mingle with the crisp packets, beer cans and sweetie papers clinging to hedges, wrapped around railings or bunched up in the gutter.

But she didn't step over it. She stood looking down at it and wondered what made a person deliberately ignore the big black local authority bin, right there on the pavement, and throw their unwanted supper into the entrance to our close. She wondered why, since the city was obviously populated by huge numbers of these persons who seemed happy to add to the large quantities of human detritus around them, the council didn't employ more street sweepers. She also wondered why it was that you never heard of somebody being fined for dropping litter. Or for letting their dog foul the pavement. And then she wondered why she was bothering to ask herself such stupid questions when she already knew the answers? Nobody cares. Nobody gives a damn. Did even she give a damn?

Having stared at the chips for longer than she really needed to, Annie came to a momentous decision. She would lift the whole mess up and deposit it in the council bin. She would never have believed herself capable of picking up someone else's rubbish, the very thought of it would once have made her feel sick. But she bent down, gingerly lifted the offending item with two fingers of each hand, and carried it the few steps to the bin at the edge of the pavement. She felt a bit embarrassed afterwards, wondering if any of the neighbours had been watching her. Silly old bat's got nothing better to do with her time now, they would think. If Joe had been alive he'd have given her a ticking off, told her she could catch all sorts from picking things up in the street. But if Joe had been alive she would probably have stepped over the chips because she wouldn't have had time to stop.

Later, when she invited me in for a cup of tea and told me all this, Annie said that she hadn't been sure what it was about that particular discarded container that had stopped her in her tracks.

"It puzzled me," she confessed. "So I went up to the church and spoke to Father Muldoon. He thought that, since it was the Monday after Easter Sunday the flesh colour of the chips and the blood red of the tomato sauce had reminded me of Christ's suffering."

Annie had liked the sound of that but, ever the realist, thought it much more likely that she had been reminded of her recently departed husband, who had split his skull when he fell, drunk, down a flight of concrete steps. I suggested that the true reason she had been forced to consider this disgusting mess on the doorstep was that now that she had no husband to run after, now that she didn't have to dash down to the butcher's to buy something for his tea, or hurry along to the newsagent's for his daily paper, she had time to stop and consider some of the more unpleasant aspects of our everyday life.

"It's a good sign," I told her. "You're moving on."

She wasn't convinced. But her initial embarrassment had obviously given way to a sense of achievement.

"I feel as if I've made a small contribution towards a cleaner world," she stated proudly. "I might even do it again some time."

And she did. She began to make a habit of lifting the odd bit of litter here and there as she walked to the shops every morning. In no time she had the close mouth clean and tidy, and had even picked up all the rubbish from below the bushes of the ground floor's front gardens – although the owners didn't seem to notice the difference since they never once mentioned it. She began to take a polythene bag with her every time she went out, so that she could lift things up from the pavement and carry them along to the nearest bin. After a while she became bolder and ventured into other close mouths, lifting soggy sheets of newspaper, twisted beer cans, bits of glass and chip wrappers. She even lifted a used condom once, though after that she began to carry a pair of rubber gloves in her pocket. She no longer worried about what the neighbours thought of her, although she was sorry that the young couple in the flat above had begun to avoid her.

"I suppose they all think I'm losing my marbles," she said.

"Not at all," I contradicted. But she was right. Comments were being made:

"Losing Joe has unhinged her."

"It's not natural, is it?"

"Oh well, as long as it keeps her happy."

Our street soon became the cleanest in the area, and the funny thing was, people stopped dropping their half finished chip suppers, or leaving their beer cans or lemonade bottles against the wall. Maybe when they saw how clean and tidy the place was they felt they didn't want to be responsible for messing it up again. It hadn't mattered so much when the place looked like a giant rubbish tip.

There was always something, of course. Usually a small piece of litter like a bus ticket, or occasionally a cigarette packet, but it didn't take Annie long to lift these few items every day. That gave her time to concentrate on other streets, then later the main road, and the shopping centre.

She became almost an institution as she walked the streets around here, looking every inch the well-dressed bag lady, rummaging here and there and stooping every so often to lift her bits and pieces.

"I have this rule," Annie told me, "that I never go back home until I've filled at least half a bag. Some days I have to walk a fair distance to find even a tiny scrap of paper, but I can usually rely on places like the cash machine at the shopping centre or the spare bit of ground at the back of the church. And there's always the mini-market and the primary school, so I'm never stuck."

It wasn't long before the local newspaper got to hear about Annie. They did an article about her and the story took up the whole of the front page. There was a big colour picture of her dropping a polystyrene container full of chips and tomato sauce into a bin. I wondered if they'd bought it specially, just for the photo, but apparently the photo-shoot was done just after lunchtime, outside the Secondary School. The photographer must have known there would be no shortage of props.

In the article she said that she liked to keep busy because it was lonely being on her own, what with her husband just passed on and her only daughter being in Australia. There was a whip-round in the newspaper office after that, and they roped in some of their advertisers, so in no time at all Annie was off down under for three weeks. She had a great time, but she said she wouldn't like to be away for so long again; she came back to an awful mess.

She was on local radio too. They had her on a phone-in programme, and a teacher phoned to ask if she'd be interested in going along to her school to talk to the children. Annie was a bit nervous about that but it was very successful. Now she's been round all the schools in the area, talking to the kids and judging anti-litter poster competitions.

"They all seem very enthusiastic, and some of them even remember not to throw their crisp bags and sweetie papers on the ground," she told the listeners when the radio station did a follow-up programme recently. "In fact, with all this publicity it's a wonder there's any litter lying around the streets in our area. But, there's always something to be lifted."

Annie's been picking up other people's rubbish for over a year now. Sometimes she finds a bit of money. Never much, just the odd one or two or five pence piece, and very occasionally a bit more, like the time she found three pound coins in the gutter outside the chip shop. She keeps it all in a box and every few months puts it in the collecting tin in the Oxfam shop. Once she found a wallet complete with credit cards and about fifty pounds in cash, but she took that to the police station. She got five pounds as a reward, and that went into the box too. She also handed in a gold crucifix and chain but she never heard any more about that.

People often stop to talk to her as she works. They ask her why she does it, what she gets out of it, and she tells tell them that she does it because it makes her happy, because she hopes it makes others happy to live in such a clean, litter-free environment. Do they want to help her? Nobody ever does.

Annie always comes out to speak to me as I'm passing her door. She's done this every day since I retired because she thinks she might persuade me to take over when she gives up. Not that she's ready to throw in the towel yet, you understand, but she's not getting any younger, and her arthritis plays up in the frosty weather.

"You could always go round with me for a while," she offered yesterday morning. "To get you used to it. There's no money in it, of course, just a clean world. But we all know cleanliness is next to Godliness so that should be reward enough. It's not always easy the first time, but it's not all that difficult either. It just requires a little bit of courage and a large amount of leg work. Good for the heart. And the soul."

"I'll think about it," I told her, then made my escape.

But a funny thing happened on the way back from the shops this morning. I saw a plastic bottle sticking out from the park railings and I couldn't help myself. I picked it up and carried it home to put in the recycling bin. I saw Annie's curtains twitching as I passed, but I pretended I hadn't seen her. I was a bit shaken though – had to pour myself a large brandy. Two actually.

I won't go out tomorrow. I've got enough food in the fridge to last till Thursday; by then I'll be back to my old self. If Annie comes to the door I'll tell her I've got flu. And when I pass her door on Thursday it'll be as if nothing has happened. If she does ask about that bottle, I'll just say it was my own, that I'd bought juice because I was thirsty and drank it on the way home. I won't get annoyed. I always try to give people their due respect, even old women who are off their trolley.

And it's important to act as if everything is normal.

Suburban Myth

There was nothing effeminate about Peregrine Prendergast. It was just that he liked sewing. Pen, as his friends called him, was excellent with a needle and thread. In fact, he was so often asked to run up a pair of curtains on his mother's old Singer, or make a dress or alter a jacket, that he wondered if he ought to give up his day job and go into business as a seamster, if that's what a male seamstress is called.

"You'll never make a living with that sewing malarkey," said his friend Andy, who was lead guitar in a group called Omega. "Come and join our band. We're looking for a drummer. You'd be good at that."

But Pen wasn't convinced.

"The sewing machine's my instrument," he said. And

he thought about the steady rhythmic rumpety-thump, rumpety-thump of his old treadle. That was his kind of music.

What Pen needed was a bit of money to set himself up, to keep the wolf from the door until the orders began to roll in, but he didn't earn much as a window cleaner. He had no savings, and being an only child, now orphaned, he had no relatives from whom he could expect an inheritance. So, short of a win on the Lottery, the Pools, or the 3.30 at Market Rasen, all of which he subscribed to on a regular basis, there was very little chance of him swapping his ladder and bucket for a digital sewing machine.

As luck would have it, Pen was cleaning the inside windows of the town hall one afternoon in preparation for a charity fashion show when one of the models, Ursula Flitt, arrived. He heard Ursula before he saw her because she was standing in the car park surrounded by cases, screaming at one of her entourage who had forgotten to pack the most important piece of luggage – the principal gown for the finale that evening.

Pen looked at the tall, slim blonde then at the midnight blue velvet curtains surrounding his now gleaming window. He ripped the curtains from their hooks, ran outside and draped the material over Ursula's neck.

"You're going to look stunning," he assured her.

Pen persuaded her to go back to his place so that he could "run her up something special". The afternoon passed in a flurry of cutting, pinning, fitting and finishing. For Pen, that is. While he made his Singer sing, the beautiful model lounged on the settee in her underwear, flicking round the TV channels. It was very distracting. At each fitting Pen tried to keep his distance, tried to avoid touching her satin-soft flesh, but Ursula pressed ever closer until, at the last fitting, she grasped his hand and slid it inside the top of the dress to demonstrate how comfortably she could breathe. He was lost.

"Does this mean we're engaged?" asked Ursula afterwards as she lounged once more on the settee.

Pen stared at her lying there, at the beautiful drape of her folds. She had obviously been seduced by the music of his machinery. He shook himself. He mustn't look or he'd never get the dress finished. He went back to work.

Ursula, although Pen would never have guessed it, was also working. She was calculating how much more money she could make in the modelling business if she had her very own, live-in dressmaker. As it was she was at the mercy of the fashion houses, who would phone her agent if they wanted her to model their clothes, then a contract would be drawn up, and fittings would begin. It all took such ages, and she wasn't getting any younger. Still, it was great what make-up could do, and she'd had no complaints about her figure. If she had someone like Pen at her beck and call she could design her own clothes, give her own shows, walk her own catwalk. And she could do it where and when she liked. Her well-paid career would become even more lucrative.

Ursula smiled lovingly at Pen and Pen smiled lovingly back. The future looked rosy.

Ursula, in her new blue velvet gown, was the star of the charity fashion show. She and Pen announced their engagement that night and they were married within the month. They rented a large empty shop and filled it with bales of cottons, velvets, silks and satins, a state-of-the-art digital sewing machine and all the other paraphernalia necessary to an up-and-coming seamster's business. Pen began by running up some new summer clothes for his lovely wife – a few dresses, skirts and slacks, a couple of light jackets – all to her own design. She looked stunning in them, which wasn't surprising, thought Pen, since she looked stunning in anything. Even in nothing at all.

Ursula persuaded Pen that the best way to advertise his services was not through the Yellow Pages as he'd suggested, but through their very own fashion show. She would design a collection and he could produce it, in her size only. She would then model the clothes, in some smart hotel full of rich ladies, and the orders would start rolling in. It would be a great success for both of them.

And a great success it was. It led to other shows in other venues, and the larger stores got to hear about them, and sent in big orders. Soon they had to buy larger premises, employ people to help with the sewing. In no time at all Pen had twelve girls working for him. The whirr of the electric machines, the rustle of silks and satins, the murmur of the girls voices were all music to his ears. A symphony of seamstresses, sewing in harmony, thought Pen. Ursula also had to employ help – a tall, tanned bodyguard called Hector who drove her around the countryside and kept the crowds of admirers at bay. Ursula told Pen he was gay.

Pen and Ursula soon became very wealthy. They bought a huge house in the best part of London that had everything they would ever need, including an enormous dressing room off the bedroom for Ursula's clothes. Pen decided that now was the time for his lovely wife to retire and drape herself elegantly once more across the sofa. He could work from home, and they could spend their days gazing longingly at one another.

Ursula wasn't really up for all that togetherness. It was all right for Pen, at least he had someone beautiful to gaze longingly at, but he didn't really have a lot going for him in the looks department. Still, she had to admit, he was clever with his hands. That's why she'd married him after all.

"If I'm going to retire," she told Pen, "I'll have to do a farewell tour."

And so it was that a tour was planned. Ursula was to take four large collections – spring, summer, autumn and winter – around America, showing the clothes each season in as many different venues as she could.

"I'll miss you my pet," Pen told her dreamily as he nuzzled into her neck, the night before she left. "Would you like me to make you something pretty while you're away? Just tell me. I can make anything you want. Anything. I could make you the moon."

Ursula thought hard. She was going to be away for quite a while, longer than Pen realised, so she'd have to keep him busy till she got back. She didn't want him getting bored and going back to his old ways, running up curtains for all and sundry. Still, the moon was a bit much.

"I'd like you to weave me a carpet for my dressing room," she replied at last. "A woollen carpet. A tartan, woollen carpet."

Pen hadn't realised that America, for Ursula, meant South as well as North. A year passed. Pen kept himself busy. He had installed a loom in the dressing room so that he wouldn't have to carry Ursula's carpet around as it became heavier, and there he worked, amongst his beloved's most treasured possessions, weaving a little each day. As the shuttle shifted backwards and forwards click-clack, click-clack, and his body swayed in time to the rhythm set by his foot on the pedals, he would hum along to whatever tune came into his head. It was always a love song.

It had taken him a while to get started on the carpet because he couldn't decide which tartan would be appropriate. There was no Clan Flitt or even Prendergast, so eventually he chose the Hunting Stewart, the tartan of royalty. It was well under way before it occurred to him that he knew nothing about Ursula's opinions on hunting. Maybe killing animals for sport wasn't quite her thing, he thought, and ripped the whole thing out. He decided the Dress Gordon might be more suitable. Hadn't she loved dancing the Gay Gordons at their wedding ceilidh. Pen sent off for wool in other colours and had completed nearly four yards before he realised that the gay connotation might be considered offensive. Pen wasn't convinced about the bronzed bodyguard's leanings, but he thought he'd better play safe. He ripped it out and started again. He had plenty of time in hand. Ursula had phoned to say that she wanted to say her farewells to Europe. Then Africa, and Asia, and Australia.

The years passed. Every so often, Ursula sent an order for new clothes or for replacements for those that had become too worn looking. Once she sent a request for some smart trousers for Hector. Pen wondered if Ursula had taken the inside leg measurement. He passed these orders on to the girls in the sewing shop, who were getting a little bored with not much work to occupy them. Pen offered to buy them some material so that they could design and make outfits for each other. They were delighted and each in turn threw her arms around him and gave him a big thank you kiss. He promised to help out with the fittings.

Meanwhile he continued to weave the carpet. He'd had to discard various tartans after he had completed a few yards – the Barclay (too yellow), the hunting and the dress Ramsay (one too red, one too blue) and the MacSporran (just too *tartan*) – but then he had discovered the Balnagown, the inoffensive brown-beige tartan that Mohammed al Fayed had commissioned for Harrods. Ursula loved shopping in Harrods, so it was very fitting, thought Pen.

Time passed. The girls from the workshop took to coming to the house to keep Pen company. Sometimes one, or even two, would stay to cook him lunch or dinner. Or breakfast. It was a happy time all things considered.

Pen couldn't remember how long Ursula had been gone, but the carpet wasn't even half finished when she finally, unexpectedly, came home. It was unfortunate that she arrived when all twelve of his employees were in the house, helping him celebrate his birthday. The scantily clad girls were dancing around the bedroom, belting out *I Will Survive* while Pen accompanied them on the loom, click-clack! click-clack-clack! click-click-clack! The noise was deafening: Ursula had to scream very loudly to get their attention. She ordered them all out of the house, and they good-naturedly danced down the stairs and out of the front door in conga fashion. Ursula thought she might sack them all in the morning.

"You should have told me you were coming," Pen told Ursula. "I could have picked you up at the airport. I suppose Hector drove you home."

"Hector's history. I had to get rid of him. He was refusing to comply." Ursula took off her coat. Pen thought she looked very smart in the dark blue shift dress he'd recently sent her. Ursula, misinterpreting his appraising look, and remembering their first meeting, slowly undressed and draped herself once again over the sofa. Except that the pose was now more of a droop, or a dangle.

Pen gazed at her in wonder. He could hardly believe that gravity could exert such a pull on a woman. Those bingo wings, where did they come from? And the chicken skin? And the crow's feet?

Ursula gazed at her husband, also in wonder. The years had been good to him, she thought. He'd obviously been taking good care of himself. He looked very trim.

"Is it time for bed?" asked Ursula.

"You go on ahead," replied Pen. And humming a little ditty, off he went to work on the carpet.

Nice Work

I hate parties. All that pretentiousness, the false pleasantries, the blatant networking. But I'd just moved to the town and didn't know anybody, so my new neighbour's birthday bash seemed as good a place as any to meet people. It's difficult for me, you see, being in a wheelchair, I don't get out as much as I'd like to. I came here to get away from my parents. They smother me. I like being independent, and I suppose I'm lucky I can hold down a job, but it's not easy. I'm not looking for sympathy though. I just want to be treated like everyone else, but that never seems to happen at parties. I'm easy prey for other lone partygoers who see me as a sitting target. If I don't get landed with somebody who spends the evening patronising me, I get somebody who takes an unhealthy interest in my disability. I've even been asked how I get onto the toilet, for God's sake! All I ask for is an intelligent conversation, but usually I'm treated as if non-working legs equal non-working brain. Still, I live in hope.

Anyway, there I was, alone, inviting "come and annoy me", when I saw an anxious looking woman heading towards me with that familiar pitying gleam in her eyes. I knew I wasn't in for a fun evening.

"Are you here on your own too?" was her opening gambit.

Useless to deny it, she was home and dry. She relaxed visibly when I confirmed her assumption.

My host had thoughtfully parked me next to an empty armchair which my new friend now settled into, making sure that she was sitting comfortably before she began. She was Elspeth, from Edinburgh, had attended a well-known private girls' school there, was unmarried but had a dog, enjoyed walking and visiting art galleries and museums, didn't know anyone at this party.

I had been plotting my escape since the girls' school, but Plan A (down drink, head off for refill) had been thwarted by the attentive host who appeared before me with a bottle of Cava even as I upended my glass). Plan B (impending migraine, leave) was beginning to shape up nicely when my new acquaintance suddenly seemed to remember that a conversation ought to be a two way process.

"And how do *you* pass your time?"

She gave me a condescending smile. I knew she didn't entertain any expectation that I might actually work, far less have a successful professional career. I toyed with the idea of telling her I was a prostitute specialising in men with unusual needs, but she didn't look the type to be shocked at that. I'd have to bore her into leaving.

"I'm a writer."

Now, it no longer surprises me that whenever I tell anyone I'm a writer they invariably come out with the "I've always wanted to write a book, I just never seem to have the time" line; but I never cease to be amazed at the lack of originality of the conversation that is sure to follow. I ask them what their book, if they had the time to write it, would be about, and after about ten seconds of shocked surprise (because they had never seriously entertained the idea in the first place) they tell me it would be a novel based on the true events of their life so far. I summarise of course. These are not the actual words used, but I'm sure you get my drift. They then begin to expound on the horrors/ happiness of their childhood in some inner city/idyllic countryside (no-one admits to the mundane suburbs), the fascinating people they have met and the hilarious anecdotes they'd like to share with the British reading public (no murders confessed, you understand, no torrid love affairs, no sadomasochistic erotic fantasies revealed).

"Of course," they usually conclude, "I'd have to disguise the characters a bit, but I'm sure it would make a great story. What do you think?"

I usually think a smile and a platitude. They don't really want an answer, just agreement.

Elspeth was no different. She prattled on until she practically glowed with the thrill of contemplating her tastefully jacketed hardback displayed invitingly on the shelves of Waterstones, until something, and it may well have been my glazed expression, brought her to a halt with the words:

"So, you're a writer."

I could tell by the slight grimace playing around her lips that she was playing for time. She was struggling to remember my name but was obviously losing the battle, and she was hoping that her statement would be interpreted as a question, accepted by me as an invitation to talk about myself. The fact that the polite preliminaries to her self-absorbed monologue hadn't included mutual introductions seemed to have escaped her.

I gave her an affirmative smile and a nod, and tossed the ball back into her court.

"What is it that you write?" she asked, inclining her question towards the general rather than the particular, not wanting to ask me directly, especially if I was a famous author, what I had actually written, because then she might have had to admit that she had never read any of my books.

Other people have used this ploy. I usually reply that I'm a general writer, and since they don't know what this is, and are too embarrassed to say so, the conversation then tails off into more mundane matters until one or other of us finds an excuse to terminate the encounter. But I had misjudged Elspeth.

"What sort of a general writer?"

This was not to be seen as an admission of ignorance on her part, only a request for elucidation. She had me cornered.

"I compose Titles," I replied.

"Titles?" Her eyebrows shot up like two question marks. I could see I wasn't going to get rid of her easily.

"Contrary to what many people believe," I said, trying not to look pointedly at her, "aspiring writers rarely make a fortune from pouring out their own autobiographical life stories. Many, of course, do it as a first work. Some astute ones even drag it out into a trilogy. But once it's written, it's written. They can't do it a second time. For subsequent books they have to become more adventurous, explore other avenues, open up their horizons if they don't want to sink into oblivion. This is where I come in. Whether they want to write romantic novels or academic textbooks, science fiction or historical drama, or even just a short story, I furnish writers with titles that they can weave their stories around."

Elspeth was obviously having difficulty getting her head around this newly introduced concept. She had been rendered speechless. I decided to take pity on her.

"Let me explain," I said, adopting the attitude of a lecturer about to expound on a complex scientific theory to a class of first year students. It's taken me years to perfect this tone. "It is not generally understood that a Title isn't merely a combination of a few words prettily joined together. It is, or should be, a succinct and appealing resumé, a précis, suggesting an outline or a summary of what is to follow. Let me give you some examples. A title such as *Nightmares in Strange Beds*, might explore the themes of fear, the past, inner journeys and so on. A title such as *Romance in Rome* would deal with love and travel. *But I Digress* would obviously suggest some well known after dinner speaker's autobiography. So you see, Title writing is the basis of Literature itself. It's an art form. Not everyone can do it."

Elspeth seemed impressed. "Is there a lot of call for Title writers?"

"Of course there is," I replied, warming to my subject. "You wouldn't believe the amount of work I get. Not just from authors either. Magazine and newspaper editors often contact me whenever they decide to run a Short

Story competition, and sometimes songwriters ask for help. And on more than one occasion I've been contacted by a film company to help them out when inspiration has failed their own experts in the field. I get a lot of work from Ministers of Religion too, although why a Sunday sermon should need a snappy title I just don't know. They've got a captive audience after all."

Elspeth's mouth was beginning to drop open, in amazement I assumed, but just in case she was trying to get a word in, I hurried on.

"I also supply Titles for dinner parties and theme nights. The murder/mystery event has, after all, become rather passé. What people want now is the chance to show off their own inventive talents and use their imaginations. So when a group of friends or acquaintances get together for a Title Dinner they all get a chance to contribute something to a collective story. I even had a young mother phone me once in desperation because she couldn't cope with the prospect of a long car journey with her three bored children fighting and squabbling in the back seat, and thought that story invention just might keep them all quiet. I felt so sorry for her that I gave her three for the price of one. Not that children's Titles are any easier, but what would you have done?"

Elspeth was trying hard to hide her astonishment. She didn't want to appear naïve, but Title writing was obviously something she wanted to learn more about.

"Does it provide a good income?"

She must have been hoping that the formality of the question would make her sound polite rather than just plain nosey.

"Well, most of my friends are astonished when they learn how much money I earn. You see, I can sell a book title outright instead of having to rely on income from the number of copies sold or the pittance from public lending rights. I'm not allowed to divulge the name of the author who has bought any particular Title, so I can't claim any credit for its subsequent success, nor can I expect remuneration from the ensuing film rights, but I make a living. A very comfortable living. I have my slack periods just like everyone else, of course. The busiest times are just after some big event, like a war or a national sporting success. There was an enormous rush after the opening of the Scottish Parliament, which was only to be expected. You'd be amazed at the number of people who came over all patriotic then, and you probably wouldn't believe me if I told you their names, even if I could."

"It sounds fascinating! Do you think I could try it?"

From the way she was leaning towards me expectantly, almost panting with excitement, I knew she wasn't referring to a hypothetical future.

"What… now?"

I had expected our conversation would trail to a polite end now that I had given a good account of myself, but Elspeth plainly had other ideas. Maybe she was planning a career change.

"You pretend to be an author," she said, on the edge of her seat with anticipation. "Give me a subject, tell me what you want to write about, and I'll think up a title."

I thought for a few moments, wondering whether to make the task so easy for her she would quickly become bored with this new game, or to make it so difficult that she would have to admit defeat. What I really wanted was for her to feel obliged to go off and find some other lone partygoer to speak to. I decided that deceptively easy might be the best tactic.

"Okay. I want to write a tourist book about Edinburgh."

She thought about this for longer than I had expected before announcing triumphantly,

"*Stay a While in the Royal Mile*".

"Mmm," I said as I clenched my teeth, trying not to laugh. It sounded like a Harry Lauder song. "Perhaps a tad location specific?"

She looked disappointed.

"Would you like to try again?"

Another few minutes passed.

"I've got it! "*Edinburgh Street by Street*". Titles were obviously not Elspeth's forte.

"Not bad," I lied graciously. "But I think you'll probably find that one's already been written. You'll have to be a bit more original."

"Well what would *you* suggest?" She sounded piqued.

"What about *Scott's City* spelt with a double "t". Sir Walter Scott's city and also a Scots, as in Scottish, city. It's a clever play on words, don't you think? And it would allow the writer to give a literary slant to his or her work, or to have an introduction dealing with Scott's connection with Edinburgh."

"You make it sound very easy," she said, then realising that I might take offence at this remark, compounded it by adding, "Easier than writing a whole book anyway. Have you ever thought of writing a whole book?"

I kept my cool. No point in reducing myself to her level.

"I've never been tempted in that direction," I replied. "Not that I have any doubts about my ability, we all have a book within us, after all. Well, some of us have. I just don't have the time. I'm a writer, yes. But I see my profession as much more prestigious than that of the author. I am the supplier rather than the retailer. The owner rather than the manager."

I could see that she was struggling to find something smart and witty to say, something clever that would allow her to have the last word before she extricated herself from our encounter with her dignity intact. But suddenly she glanced at her watch and stood up.

"Sorry, your time's up," she announced with a bright smile.

"What?"

"Your time's up," she repeated. "I'm only supposed to give thirty minutes to each of you. You're over that already."

"What do you mean 'thirty minutes each'? What are you talking about?"

Elspeth radiated smugness.

"I'm paid by the half hour, you see." And since I obviously didn't see, she explained. "I'm a professional partygoer. I'm paid to make conversation with the guests. I don't have to talk to them all, of course, just the ones that no-one else is talking to. The wallflowers. Well…it's been lovely meeting you."

And with that she turned and strode purposefully towards the opposite side of the room where a studious looking young man stood examining a shelf full of books.

As I said, I hate parties.

Early One Morning

When Lizzie's father collapsed at the table clutching at his chest early one frosty winter's morning, barely managing to gasp out a plea for help before vomiting his breakfast back onto his plate Lizzie, only eight years old, knew exactly what to do. She dialled 999, explained the emergency, gave her full name and address and, in case that wasn't enough, instructions on how to get to their isolated cottage and, while waiting for help to arrive, mopped her father's brow with a cold cloth. She even, her grandmother would boast later, went with him in the ambulance to the hospital (although really this was because the ambulance driver didn't want to leave her alone at home.) Everyone was so proud of her. If her mother had been alive she would have been proud of her too.

"If you hadn't acted so quickly your Daddy might have died," Lizzie's grandmother told her when she came to the hospital that afternoon to pick her up. She had cried then, big wet sobs as she buried her face in Granny's soft coat, and she had been cuddled and comforted.

"It's okay to cry, darling. You've been so brave today."

And her grandmother, sure that Lizzie was thinking of her mummy who had never come home from hospital, added:

"Daddy will be back home with you again very soon."

Which had made her cry even more. Lizzie wondered if she should tell Granny that she didn't want to have Daddy back home. That she didn't like Daddy sometimes. That he scared her. She wanted to explain why, but didn't know what words to use. And Granny was a grown-up, like Daddy. Would she say Lizzie was being silly or nasty or spiteful? Just because Daddy came into bed at night with her sometimes. Just for a hug. A squeeze. A kiss. That's what daddies do with their little girls, Granny would say. Touch and kiss. Your daddy loves you, that's why he does that.

Lizzie's father had stayed in hospital for nearly three weeks. Three weeks of blissful happiness for Lizzie who couldn't bear to think about what would happen when her grandmother went away.

"Please take me home with you, Granny. I'd be such a good help to you, I promise. You must be so lonely living all alone. I could keep you company."

But Granny had told her how much she would hate living in the city when she was used to the countryside, and how she would miss all her school friends, and how lonely her daddy would be without her. And then Daddy came back from the hospital, and soon after that Granny went home.

When Lizzie's father had his second heart attack, she acted just as swiftly as she had done four years before. It was early in the morning again, but this time he had finished his breakfast and was in the small toilet by the back door. He just managed to call out her name before collapsing onto the floor, where he lay, groaning, trousers round his ankles, wedged between the door and the toilet bowl.

Lizzie couldn't open the door, so she took a kitchen chair outside and climbed up onto it to look in through the small, open window. Her father's face, pressed against the cold floor, looked ghostly white, and he was sweating profusely. There was no noise coming from his slack mouth now, but she knew he was still alive because his eyes were opening and closing, as if that was the only painless movement he was able to make. Then they fixed on to her at the window, staring.

Staring at her standing there in her thin, nylon nightie. The nightie that had been her mother's. He had told her to wear it because she looked so like her mother. Her warm, beautiful mother. Lizzie clutched her arms across her chest and shivered.

She jumped down from the chair and ran back into the house. She knew about the pills he kept in his jacket pocket, and how important it was to get one into his mouth quickly. So she knew exactly what to do.

Her father's jacket was hanging over a chair in the hall, and she quickly found the bottle of pills. There were only six left.

Lizzie tipped the six pills into her hand and put the empty bottle back into the jacket pocket. She went into the kitchen, poked the pills down through the sink drain, and turned on the cold tap to flush them away. Then she got washed and dressed for school. It was almost eight o'clock. She didn't feel like eating breakfast, but she poured herself a glass of milk and put a couple of biscuits into her schoolbag, in case she got hungry later. There was no sound from the toilet as she tiptoed past and slipped out of the back door to bring in the kitchen chair.

It was a long walk to the main road to catch the school bus, but Lizzie didn't mind. She had done it before, often, because her father worked on a farm, and sometimes, especially on early spring mornings like this, he would be off at the lambing. He didn't always drive her to the bottom of the lane. So nobody would be surprised when she told them, later, that she hadn't seen her father that morning, that he hadn't woken her before he left, but anyway, she always set her own alarm clock so that she wouldn't be late for school.

Somebody from the farm would ring up to find out why her father hadn't turned up for work, but there would be nobody to answer the phone. They would be annoyed, but she didn't think they would come looking for him. He was always taking time off without telling them beforehand. That was why he had to change his job so often.

It would be a big shock for Lizzie, finding her father dead when she got home from school, but she would be very brave. She would keep calm, just as she had done before. She would dial 999 and give her name and address, and instructions on how to get to the cottage. She would phone her grandmother, who would be very proud of her.

The bus would be along soon. Lizzie looked around her at the familiar patchwork of fields with their crops and cows and sheep, at the fences and gates and gorse hedges, and at the crows flying overhead. She wondered what it would be like living in the city.

Trout

Adam was floating on his back in ten inches of heavily salted water, trying to think pleasant thoughts, when the idea came to him. He had been told by the therapist that one of the benefits of a session in the flotation tank would be deep mental relaxation, an emptying of the mind, yet his brain had been working overtime on all sorts of worries and anxieties: such as how he would manage to find the door when it was time to leave this blacked-out cell. He imagined he'd have to stand up and reach out till he made contact with a wall, then move along the surface testing it with both hands – a bit like Britt Ekland in that bedroom scene in *The Wicker Man* – until he came upon the door handle.

There was also the problem of what to do with his arms. At the moment he had his hands clasped behind his head, which was fairly comfortable, but he couldn't keep them like that for the full hour or they'd become stiff and sore. He had tried relaxing them by his sides, but the buoyancy of the water floated them out sideways until his elbows were level with his ears and his forearms dangled in the general direction of his hips. He was tempted to stretch them straight out at right angles to his body and cross his legs at the ankles, but he thought that might be blasphemous. He supported his head again with his hands. He was anything but relaxed.

Then there was the hygiene issue. Adam couldn't help thinking about all the bodies that had been floating in the tank before him that day: had they all washed thoroughly first? Was he floating in a pool of dirt and germs, not to mention hair and dead skin cells? The leaflet he had read in the waiting room suggested that the enormous quantity of Epsom Salts in the water would draw toxins out of his body. Where would these toxins go? Was he, in fact, lying there absorbing the toxins of those who had been in there before him? He was sorry he had allowed Marissa to talk him into this so-called therapy.

"They say it works wonders for anxiety," she had told him. "And depression. It's just what you need."

Adam wondered who "they" were. Here he was, anxious about being in the tank, anxious about how clean it was, anxious about getting out of it, depressed about not enjoying it and depressed about the thought of having to lie there being anxious for an hour. It wasn't working, was it? "They", it seemed, were wrong.

He toyed with the idea of standing up and finding his way out of this oversized coffin, but Marissa was out there, in the next room, having a facial. She would hear the shower running; she would probably even hear him trying to find his way out of the tank. She had that super-acute, finely-tuned hearing that only a wife can possess. Sometimes he was sure she could hear him thinking.

It was Marissa's discriminating hearing that had caused his anxiety and depression in the first place. No, that wasn't fair. He couldn't lay this one on Marissa's shoulders. It was his own faulty hearing; dare he say it, even to himself? His own deafness. He just couldn't be deaf. For a musician in an orchestra, of course, deafness was an occupational hazard: a lot of them became deaf to a greater or lesser degree sooner or later, what with all the noise going on around them all the time. But he was a concert pianist, for God's sake. It wasn't expected.

It had taken him a long time to admit he had a problem. About the beginning of last year, when he was practising for a concert in Dubai, he began to notice a change in the tone of his piano and wondered if it was suffering the effects of the previous two extremely damp summers. When he mentioned this to Marissa she insisted that the piano sounded as good as it always had. She had a good ear, so she ought to have noticed there was something odd about the sound. He had wondered if perhaps she was becoming a little dull of hearing. She was, after all, approaching fifty. Later that year, when Erica came home from South America, en route for Budapest, and unpacked her violin so that they could play a duet together, he was horrified to hear the mistakes she made. She was usually note perfect. Lack of practice, he supposed, because of her busy lifestyle; but when he suggested this to her she became extremely stroppy.

"There's nothing wrong with my playing," she shouted as she flounced out of the room to complain to her mother. "Why don't you get yourself a hearing aid?"

Marissa, who had been listening from the kitchen, took Erica's side.

"I thought she played the piece perfectly," she said. "Maybe you should get your ears syringed. Shall I make an appointment for you?"

He had refused, of course. But gradually all the little bits of the jigsaw had clicked together: the tone of the piano;

not hearing Erica's high notes; the television sounding muffled; even thinking the musicians who occasionally accompanied him sometimes sounded a bit off. It shouldn't matter, Adam thought. Beethoven managed to keep going when he was deaf. But he wasn't Beethoven. If he made a mistake while practising, how would he know? It wasn't just a case of hitting the right keys; he had to hear the tone, the nuances. He supposed it meant his career was over.

Marissa had been sympathetic, but pragmatic.

"Well, it's not the end of the world. Just be thankful you can afford to retire. And think of all the things we can do: we can spend the whole winter in Sitges, visit my family in Chisinau, go up to Edinburgh and stay with Oliver and Patrick. We'll have a wonderful time."

Adam no longer even liked Sitges, which had become overcrowded with tourists since they had bought the house there. He'd rather cut his wrists than spend time with her mad Moldovan relatives, and so far he had managed to avoid sleeping in the same house as Oliver and his partner. It wasn't that he didn't love his son, and he accepted the situation, of course he did, but it was all so... oh, he didn't know what it was.

"It's not as if you're completely deaf," said Marissa. "You'll still be able to enjoy life."

Yes, but for how long? He'd soon have to get a hearing aid. Maybe two. What if he reached the stage where he couldn't hear anything at all? How would he cope? He became quite agitated. He didn't want to be deaf. He didn't want to retire. How could he live without his music? He couldn't sleep, went off his food. That was when Marissa dragged him along to the Health Oasis, to relax in the flotation tank.

Adam tried not to think about his encroaching deafness, and instead worried about how much longer he would have to spend floating in this black hole. He was surprised he didn't feel cold lying in the water. There would be a system for maintaining the temperature, no doubt, like in swimming pools, with air filters, with droplets of water dripping from them. He'd probably end up in hospital with Legionnaire's disease. Or at the very least get an ear infection. He wished he'd remembered to put in the foam earplugs that had been given to him. He tried to focus on emptying his mind, but found that impossible, so he began to imagine himself playing one of his favourite pieces of music – one of the variations on a theme from Schubert's "Trout" Quintet: the one where the double bass carries the melody as the pianist gives a virtuoso performance on the keyboard. He took his hands from behind his head to play the notes into the air, and it was at this moment that he became aware of the silence. He could hear nothing. Nothing. He was conscious of his heart pounding in his ears, but that was more a sensation than a sound. And then, in that complete silence, as he played his piano in the air, he could hear the notes. He could hear them in his head as his fingers rippled along the keys, hear the double bass by his side. Yes. He could hear the music perfectly.

And that was when the idea came to him. It was as if a switch had been flicked; he could almost see a little light bulb going on inside his head, illuminating his brainwave.

He would give a concert. A piano recital, but with a difference. An air piano recital. And why not? Plenty of people played air guitar didn't they? There was even a World Air Guitar Championship Competition; he'd seen an article about it in the newspaper. Well he would play air piano. He would perform a whole concerto facing his audience with his imaginary instrument, and they, instead of hearing the music in the traditionally accepted manner, would interpret the sounds as he expressed them through his hands, his face, his head, his whole body. Goodness, he could think of pieces he could interpret with just his eyebrows. It would be a concert for the deaf principally – from the hard of hearing to the profoundly deaf – but anyone would be able to come along. It seemed such a simple idea he wondered it hadn't been done before; or perhaps it had and he hadn't heard about it. In fact, he could probably get a little group together, a trio perhaps, or even a quintet sometimes – he'd need a quintet for "The Trout". He thought about the dozens of musicians he knew, some of them old friends. Like Peter. He could ask Peter to be violin; he had the most expressive face Adam had ever seen. Peter would be happy to help out. And Sam – double bass would have to be Sam. With his long face and large watery eyes he'd be ideal; and he had retired last year, so he was sure to be bored by now. Then there was Sam's wife, Stella. She played the cello, he remembered; she hadn't played professionally for years, so she'd probably be happy to be asked. That just left the viola. Maybe Marissa would do that – she used to be quite good, just needed a little practice; anyway, it wasn't as if anybody would notice if she dropped a note here and there. It was only the viola after all. Marissa certainly knew how to convey what she wanted to say with just a look, so he didn't think she'd have much problem with musical expression.

His mind raced on, working out a programme, deciding which venue would be most appropriate, wondering about Arts Council funding, till the piercing strains of a Peruvian flute filtered into the chamber, breaking into his deliberations and signalling the end of his session. Adam stretched out an arm and his hand immediately came into contact with the door handle. He pulled himself up, pushed open the door and stepped out into the dimly lit shower area.

"*And here and there he da-a-arted, as swift as swi-ift could be.*" He sang loudly as he stood under the hot water, scrubbing the salt out of his hair. "*Was never fish so li-ively, and frolicsome as he?*"

He hoped Marissa could hear him.

You've Got to Laugh

She's toddling along beside me as we make our way down Sauchiehall Street, I turn to fend off a woman doing market research for some catalogue, and when I look round she's gone.

I try not to panic. She's done this before. I know she'll either be in Boots or Marks and Spencer's because they've both got escalators. Marks is nearest so I run in there, and sure enough there she is at the foot of the escalator, leaning over at a funny angle with her hand outstretched.

"Mother!"

But I'm not in time to stop her pushing the button. A dozen bodies lurch forward as they come to a sudden halt, but nobody falls. I grab her arm and drag her away while they're all still standing there, looking around them as if they've just wakened from some hypnotic trance and are trying to work out where they are.

I don't know why she does it and I don't suppose she knows either. Maybe she used to do it because she was scared to step onto a staircase that was moving, so she learned how to make it stop. But that was when she was what you might call semi-rational. When she did silly things but you could work out the reasoning behind them. Nowadays she doesn't even bother to go up or down the stairs once they've stopped moving. She just presses the button and stands there grinning, as if she'd been told the funniest joke. Mind you, you've got to laugh when you see all these people as the stairs come to a sudden halt and they keep going, grabbing onto each other as they try to keep their balance.

I hustle her out of the shop back onto Sauchiehall Street. I don't like being in shops with her, it makes me nervous. And I'm not just talking about the escalators. If we stop beside a display with something on it that takes her fancy, her hand shoots out like a snake's tongue and it's in her pocket. How can someone who is so slow of thought be so quick of movement? I have to keep my eyes on her the whole time. It's become a joke with her granddaughters, if they want some make-up or jewellery that they can't afford.

"Can we take Granny shopping?" they'll say.

I keep her close and point things out in the shop windows till we reach Buchanan Street. I wish I'd brought the car. There's an hour to wait till the train leaves, so I take her into a café for something to eat. We've only been out together half a day and already I feel frazzled. I used to enjoy a trip into town with her, having coffee or lunch, chatting about this and that. Now it's just a question and answer session:

"What would you like to eat?"

"Beans"

"They don't have beans here. What about a cake?"

"Why don't they have beans?"

"Because they only have cakes."

"I want beans."

We've been down this path before, in other cafés, so I know just how long we might be talking about beans. And all the while she has a smile on her face like the sun coming out.

I order cake and tea. She puts the whole slice into her mouth but it's too big to chew, so she starts to laugh. She takes it out again and has a slurp of tea. She's like a toddler, learning to feed herself – mashed up cake in one hand, wobbly cup in the other.

This regression into a sort of geriatric childhood will continue until she can no longer walk or talk, and she'll need to wear nappies and be fed with thickened liquids and spend most of her days asleep. The doctor told me that. He also told me I should put her into a care home now, before I become unable to cope. Easy for him to say. It's not his mother. But I've agreed to have a look at some places, see which one I'd prefer. She'd prefer. I wonder whether, if our roles were reversed, if she was healthy and I needed to be cared for, she would put me in a home. Somehow I don't think so. My mother would look after me. I suspect mothers love their children more than children love their mothers.

She's licking her fingers, and as I catch her eye she beams another smile at me. I should be glad that she doesn't suffer, that she has no awareness of what's happening to her, but I feel frustrated, and angry, and helpless, for her as well as me. I can do nothing to stop her downward spiral, but I must try to keep her with me, with her family who love her, as long as I can. I smile back at her.

"Come on, Mum," I say as I wipe her hands clean. "It's time to go home."

Sarah's in the kitchen stirring at a pasta sauce when we get back. I can tell by her quiet, resigned smile that there's been an argument with her sister about who should cook dinner. They're both in the middle of exams, but Alanna's, being finals, are deemed more important – by Alanna. I want to shake her and tell her to stop being so self-centred; I want to shake Sarah and tell her not to give in so easily. Instead I sniff the air:

"Smells delicious, doesn't it, Mum? Spaghetti Bolognese. Your favourite."

We all laugh, including my mother, who almost certainly doesn't remember the last time we ate spaghetti: before I'd had time to cut it up for her she had pulled it out from under its sauce and tried to untangle it like a ball of wool before depositing it under the table.

"I think I'll get Granny to lie down for an hour. I'll feed her later."

"Maybe I should have made something else..."

"It's not the spaghetti. Really. Granny's tired, that's all. It's been a long day for her."

It's been a long day for me too. I just want to put my mother into another room, out of my sight, so that I can be normal for a while, with my girls. An hour of freedom. Maybe I could stretch it to two.

"Come on Granny. Beddy-byes." Alanna has taken her grandmother's hand and is leading her out of the kitchen.

"Beddy." She laughs as she totters along behind Alanna, and we all laugh with her.

Over dinner I tell the girls about the incident with the escalator in Marks and Spencer.

"Mega embarrassment" says Alanna.

"Poor Granny." Sarah looks tearful. "It's just not fair."

No, it's not fair. But there's no court I can petition for a more just treatment in this scheme of things, no judge who'll decree that my mother's mind, her spirit, her very essence must be restored to us. I know I'll never get my mother back. But I won't let this sadness take hold.

"Do you remember the time she put those tins of tuna fish in her pocket at the supermarket? And the bottle of perfume in Boots? And those Christmas decorations?"

I continue to reminisce, leaving out the sad bits, the bad bits, and the girls are laughing, throwing in their tuppenceworth, not wanting to be outdone.

"And that time she put the ice cream cone in her handbag? We didn't notice that till it started dripping out of the bag and down her skirt."

"And remember when I took her for a walk in the Botanic Gardens, and she picked one of the best plants in the Orchid House? We had to make a quick exit."

Our supply of anecdotes is soon exhausted, but we move easily on to other topics so that by the time dinner is over Granny is no longer uppermost in our minds. I shoo them both off to their rooms to study, and am gathering up the dishes when I hear a scream.

"No, Granny. No!"

"Mum! Mum!" Sarah sounds distraught.

They're in my bedroom; my mother is standing at the bottom of my bed, in a tangle of underwear and a pool of diarrhoea. Alanna is holding her by the wrists.

"I tried to stop her. It's all over her hands."

Sarah looks as if she might faint. My mother smiles up at Alanna and tries to pull her hands away.

"She must have been trying to get to the loo."

"Run a bath for Granny, will you Sarah?" I try to sound calm and controlled, and force myself to smile back at my mother. "Let's get you in the tub. You like a nice warm bath don't you?"

She's still smiling as Alanna leads her towards the door.

"Bet you're glad you put in that laminate flooring," says Alanna, and we both laugh.

You've got to laugh. Haven't you.

Hotel Riposo

Doreen wasn't happy. At her bidding, the receptionist had sent for 'someone with more authority' and Robert could sense his wife girding her loins for battle as the young manager, in stylish jacket, open-necked shirt and tight jeans, now approached.

"I am Fabio." He smiled all over them and shook their hands as if they were long lost friends. "What seems here the problem? You do not like your room?"

"It's not what we paid for," said Doreen, who always spoke for both of them. "We were supposed to have a balcony."

Fabio swiped a sleepy cat from the desk and consulted the computer.

"I apologise deeply," he said, "but there is not an empty room with a balcony."

Doreen stood her ground.

"Well that's just not good enough. The room you've given us is far too small, and the bedroom's very dark. There's only one small light – how am I supposed to put my make-up on? And we asked for a walk-in shower. I can't clamber over a bath that high." She paused to think of what else she could add. "And there are only four coat hangers in the wardrobe. What use is that to anyone staying a fortnight?"

They were only staying a week, but Fabio politely overlooked this small error. He reached down behind the desk and brought up a small handful of assorted coat hangers.

"Problem solved, no?" He gave a satisfied grin.

Doreen's left eyebrow shot up – always a dangerous sign.

"We want a better room," she said emphatically, snatching the hangers from the desk. "Don't we Robert?"

Robert nodded but kept schtum. He usually said the wrong thing anyway.

Fabio sighed, defeated. He consulted his computer again.

"Ah! I have a very special room which is for families available. A very large room. But I am happy for you to use my families room if you wish," he said proudly – though whether he was proud of finding a solution to the problem, or of his language skills, which were considerable, wasn't clear. His English was certainly miles better than their Italian.

"No balcony for families though," he added.

They followed him, Doreen panting in the heat, along a corridor and up one flight of stairs, where he opened Room 101 with a flourish.

It was indeed a large room. It was enormous – with a king-sized bed as well as a small double and two single ones.

"Italians are very large in families," explained Fabio.

Doreen opened the door of a huge wardrobe where two coat hangers kept company with a spare pillow. She hung up the ones she held in her hand – now there were six.

Fabio threw open the door to the bathroom, and pressed a switch.

"You see? Lights."

He said this with an air of superiority, as if these were some newly invented contraptions exclusive to this hotel. There were indeed lights – one on each of three walls, four set into the ceiling and one above the wash hand basin.

"It's like Blackpool Illuminations," Robert joked.

Fabio smiled in agreement, taking it as a compliment. Doreen glowered at them both and went back to the wardrobe.

"Coat hangers." She spoke slowly, pointing at the existing ones. "Not enough for my clothes. Com-pren-dey."

"Si si si Signora. You want hanging. No problems."

Robert thought he detected a smirk as the manager left the room.

By evening Doreen had an upset tummy and couldn't face dinner. She blamed it on the meal they'd had on the aeroplane. Robert felt he should keep his wife company so went out and bought himself a sandwich and some wine to take back to the room.

The following day might have passed peacefully for Robert, in the garden perhaps, reading his book; but he had to minister to Doreen who was still feeling a bit seedy. He sat reading at the window overlooking the lake during the short periods when his wife was asleep, and tried not to feel put upon.

On Sunday Doreen was quite well again, and on the way back from breakfast noticed that a large party of Italian guests were checking out. She sent Robert to persuade Fabio into moving them to a now vacant room with a balcony and walk-in shower.

Fabio produced some more coat hangers from beneath the desk as soon as he saw Robert approaching.

"Women, eh?" said Robert. Fabio smiled in sympathy. He gave Robert the key to a Balcony Suite.

On Monday, Doreen sat on their large balcony sunbathing until the heat defeated her. Robert, who had enjoyed a few lengths of the pool, suggested a swim to cool her down, but she was put off by the few insects and leaves floating on top. Instead they had a walk around the air conditioned shopping centre. In the afternoon a boat trip on the lake went fairly smoothly – apart from the incident with a German tourist who had the audacity to try to board the ferry in front of Doreen.

"There's a queue," she told him indignantly, indicating the crowd behind them with one arm and elbowing him in the ribs with the other while encouraging her husband: "Come on Robert! Just push them out the way. Give them a taste of their own medicine."

Robert was relieved she didn't mention the war.

On Tuesday morning Doreen persuaded Fabio to let her use his phone to make an urgent call, because mobile coverage in the hotel was "disgraceful". She wanted to speak urgently to her friend Myra, who had promised to find out for her who was going to judge the baking at the County Show on Saturday. She needed to know, because she had to think about whether to enter the Victoria sponge category (always a safe bet if a woman was judging), or concentrate on her famous Dundee cake if the judge was male. Myra hadn't managed to find out, which put Doreen into a tizz for the rest of the day.

At dinner she complained to the waiter about the excess of pasta on the menu.

"It's not healthy, you know. All that carbohydrate."

They had planned a bus trip to the Dolomites on Wednesday, but Doreen had heard from another guest that it was freezing cold up in the mountains, and that they'd only managed one comfort stop on the four hour journey to get there, so they cancelled. Doreen spent most of the day fretting over the Dundee cake or Victoria sponge decision.

"If I lose on points this year it'll be Myra's fault," she said.

"Why not make both?" said Robert, reasonably. "We'll be home early enough. You'll have plenty of time."

"Plenty of time? Huh! That's just like a man! You've no idea, have you?"

"Try to stop worrying," said Robert. "Relax. You're on holiday. Enjoy yourself."

"I am enjoying myself," Doreen yelled.

Thursday was "Gala Night" – a farewell dinner for the many guests who, like Doreen and Robert, would leave the following morning. Drinks and nibbles were served in the garden, and this was followed by a very generous six course meal with wine. There was a singer to entertain them.

"This prosecco's too fizzy," said Doreen.

"I think it's quite delicious," said Robert.

Doreen frowned and swatted at the air in front of her face.

"Mosquitoes! You'd think the Italians would have learned how to deal with them by now. They've had them long enough."

"They're part of the food chain," said Robert, bravely. "Like our midges. You see, if you get rid of them, what will the..."

"That's right. Take their side. Why must you be so contrary?"

"Let's go in and have dinner," said Robert.

As they worked their way through the delicious meal, Robert's attention was drawn to the number of couples, probably married couples, who sat at their meal not speaking. He wondered if this was because they had long since run out of things to say to one another, or if they were just so comfortable in each other's company that they could sit happily in mutual silence. He didn't have that luxury; Doreen's voice was like a wasp in his ear:

"I don't know why he's singing Neapolitan songs. This isn't Naples."

"More pasta! Can't they think of anything else for a second course."

"That music's far too loud. I can't hear myself speak."

Robert lay awake that night, sorry that the holiday had come to an end, but glad too because he'd found the week quite stressful. He knew that Doreen couldn't help herself. She had always been a glass half empty person. In the early days of their relationship he thought he'd be able to fill that other half, and he had succeeded, up to a point. He had made her happy for a time, and she hadn't always expected the worst. Until the worst happened. Three times. Baby after baby lost before the pregnancy was established. The realisation that there would be no children. Thirty years, and Doreen hadn't really got over it. He still tried sometimes to refill her glass – but she always managed to knock it over, spill the contents. Now he mostly just tried to take care of his own glass.

He must try to clear his mind, he thought, and get off to sleep; their flight wasn't until lunchtime, but they would get up for an early breakfast then pack before heading to the airport. He was remembering that he would have to ask Fabio to organise a taxi when he felt a sharp pain shooting across his chest. This subsided quickly, but was replaced by a heaviness, as if a weight had been placed on top of him; but this too subsided and he was left with a general feeling of discomfort. Realising he was now sweating profusely, he threw off the sheet that covered him. The pain came back, this time spreading out across his left shoulder.

"Doreen," he called weakly. Then louder: "Doreen!"

"Oh for goodness sake, what is it? I've just managed to get off to sleep, and you know we've got to..."

He grasped her arm tightly, to shut her up.

"I think I'm having a heart attack."

The ambulance whisked him off to hospital where wires attached him to various machines. Doreen was allowed a few minutes with him, then was asked to wait in a side room with Fabio, who had very kindly driven her to the hospital. Robert hoped she hadn't spent the journey complaining about his driving.

An hour later the doctor was able to tell Robert that his heart was in perfect working order – so far.

"You are suffering from indigestion, probably compounded by stress. I spoke with your friend Fabio. He tells me your stay has not been a restful one. What you really need, Signore, is a holiday."

"But I am on holiday, Doctor."

"Mmm... well I think to be on the safe side we need to keep you here for observation. Stress can lead to a heart attack, and I would not like to let you go home too quickly."

"But our flight's due to leave..."

"You see, you are becoming overwrought. Please calm down. Everything will be taken care of."

The doctor explained to Robert exactly what the week's observation would entail.

Robert slept for a few minutes. When he woke, a slightly subdued Doreen was sitting beside him. It had all been arranged, she told him. Fabio would take her to the airport in the morning. She'd be home in time to bake both cakes for the competition.

"You don't mind, do you Robert? Only they said you would be fine, not a heart attack anyway, but they want you to stay for a while, the doctor says it's for the best. Fabio says he'll make sure you're looked after." She paused, thoughtful. "That was kind of him, wasn't it?"

For a moment Robert saw a glimpse of the old Doreen. No point in telling her that on his way back from the airport Fabio would call into the hospital to collect him, take him back to the Hotel Riposo where, it had been agreed, he would spend a week of rest and relaxation. Recovering his equilibrium, as the doctor so quaintly put it.

He kissed Doreen goodbye and wished her luck with the competition. Not that she needed luck, he added, since she was the best baker in the village.

"I hope you'll be okay without me," she said.

Robert gave her a reassuring smile.

"Of course I will. I'll be just fine. Really."

And he really would.

NEVERTHELESS

I have decided," said Julia, clasping her book to her chest, "to embrace death."

Charlie lowered his newspaper slightly and looked at her over the top of his glasses.

"Is there something I should know?"

"Just that death is our only certainty." She paused for effect. "It could come calling at any time."

"You've only sprained your ankle," said Charlie, going back to his reading. "And *I'm* feeling just dandy, thank you very much."

"We don't think enough about death, "said Julia, as she lifted her good leg up onto the settee and wriggled into a more comfortable position.

"Oh, I know you don't have to dwell on it *all* the time, or get depressed about it. Nevertheless, you should be aware that your time on this earth is limited; and if you keep that to the forefront of your mind, you'll do things now instead of putting them off till later. Because later might just be too late."

"Is that *you* as in *me*?"

"Don't be facetious, Charlie. It's you as in all of us. Everybody."

"Did you read that in that book?"

"Not in those words exactly." Julia examined the front cover of the little volume, as if to check, then hugged it again. "It was about a man who spent most of his time working." She paused to see if this had hit its mark, but the newspaper didn't so much as flicker. "He didn't spend much time with his family because he was working hard to save up for his retirement..."

"Very admirable."

"... so he didn't get to see all the places he and his wife had talked about visiting. He kept promising they'd do these things once he retired."

"Very sensible."

"Only, on the very day he gave up work he was diagnosed with a brain tumour and told he only had weeks to live."

"That was bad luck."

"Yes, wasn't it? He died with lots of regrets: all the people he hadn't kept in touch with, all the places he and his wife hadn't visited..."

"Are you angling for a holiday?" Charlie folded up the paper he wasn't being allowed to read. "Is that what this is about?"

A holiday would be nice, thought Julia.

"I'm just pointing out that life is short," she said, struggling up to a standing position. "And I'm going to keep that thought at the front of my mind, so that I do all the things I want to do before it's too late." She hobbled towards the door clutching her book. "And you should do the same."

Julia was glad she'd had that little conversation with Charlie, because only a week later he began having problems in the trouser department. It was unlikely to be anything serious because Charlie had a medical at work every year, and the last one was only two months before. Nevertheless, Julia made an appointment for him with their GP, who recommended further investigations.

It took two weeks for Charlie to be called to the hospital. Julia thought this had been a reasonable time to wait, given the problems of the NHS, but Charlie had complained daily; and it had given him time to worry, allowing his hypochondria mode to kick in and produce all sorts of side effects from his yet undiagnosed condition. After the biopsy he complained of a headache, a backache, and he "felt a bit dizzy". He thought he might spend the rest of the day in bed.

"It was worse than childbirth that examination," said Charlie.

"How would you know?" said Julia. "Don't be such a wimp."

Nevertheless, she put a hot water bottle in the bed for him and brought him a couple of paracetamols and some tea and toast.

The nevertheless rule loomed large in Julia's life. She liked to weigh up the alternatives, keep her options open; it was a sort of emotional insurance policy. She'd recently read that one of her favourite authors had converted to Catholicism on the nevertheless principle. Julia was impressed.

Charlie was a more resolute sort of person; he made his decisions and rarely wavered. But now, as he waited for the results of the biopsy, he seemed to do nothing but think. Never talkative at the best of times, he was even quieter than usual. He didn't attend to the garden or go to the golf club; he hardly looked at the newspaper – said he couldn't concentrate. He spent most of his time in front of the television, not really seeing what was on the screen. Julia knew he was worrying, but he wouldn't talk to her about it. She was glad her ankle had healed; she wouldn't have been able to rely on him to help around the house or do the shopping. One afternoon she found him watching a repeat of Masterchef; Charlie had no interest in cookery.

"You're wasting your life," said Julia. "You can't recover time. Once the day is gone that's it – you can't get it back."

"When did you become such a bloody philosopher?" Charlie replied.

But he knew she was right. His life was seeping away as he sat there. And what if the biopsy result was okay? He'd wasted all those days. But what if it wasn't okay? What then? What would he want to do with his last years? He couldn't think of anything special. And what would be the point of doing anything at all? He wouldn't remember it. He'd be dead.

He changed channels a few times and stopped at a wildlife programme. It was about Africa, about the wild animals that were in danger of dying out there because of illegal hunting. He'd seen some of these animals in the zoo, but never in their natural habitat. He'd probably never get the chance now. Maybe they should go on holiday to Africa. A safari. Julia would love that, he supposed. He'd always fancied a safari but thought they were too expensive to consider. They had more than enough money in the bank – what was he saving up for anyway? So that the kids could go on safari with their inheritance?

Julia was rather taken aback when Charlie suggested it to her. It was the last kind of holiday she would have considered – all that sleeping in tents, the insects, the danger. Nevertheless, it was a holiday. Gift horse and all that. And the idea seemed to be lifting him from his depressed fug. He became quite animated about the prospect of seeing elephants and rhinoceros and lions in the wild.

"I'll have a look online tomorrow" she said.

It was almost by chance that Julia came upon the luxury version of the safari holiday. She had trawled through dozens of websites promising 'unique' experiences. They all sounded much the same to her – and not very tempting. She shuddered at the thought of sleeping in a tent surrounded by claustrophobic netting; nor did she fancy fighting for position in a convoy of uncomfortable jeeps. But she didn't want to let Charlie down. She wondered if there was a better kind of safari experience, and typed this into Google. Up popped ten nights in South Africa, in a well-appointed lodge, overlooking a private lake in the grounds of a five star hotel, complete with swimming pool and spa – and with private tours of the Kruger. It was ridiculously expensive.

Julia clicked through the pages of the hotel admiring the dining areas, the lodges with their pristine looking bed linen, the lake surrounded by flowers and trees, the comfortable pop-top 4x4s. It would cost more than they'd ever paid for a holiday.

Nevertheless, it would be the most amazing experience, the holiday of a lifetime, just what the doctor ordered, so to speak. She was sure she could conjure up a few more clichés that might persuade her husband to her way of thinking. She went downstairs and made him a cup of his favourite coffee.

Charlie listened attentively as Julia, emphasising the top end transport arrangements, tried to sell him the luxury safari. To her amazement he seemed to be nodding in agreement.

"So, all things considered," she finished, "I think it would be money well spent. No pockets in a shroud."

"You're right," said Charlie. "We don't want to be the richest..."

He was interrupted by the doorbell. It was the postman with a package too large for the letterbox, and a long white envelope. A letter from the hospital.

Charlie tore it open.

"Enlarged Prostate. Benign," he shouted, hugging Julia. "Blood tests negative. There's nothing wrong with me! Can you believe it?"

"All that worrying for nothing," Julia said as she hugged him back. "I'm so glad. You still want to go on that holiday though, don't you?"

The pause was just a few seconds too long.

"There's no rush now," said Charlie.

Nevertheless... thought Julia, as she headed back upstairs to switch on the computer.

The Kiss

I am not a silly old woman. I want you to know that, because what I am about to tell you will seem so unbelievable you will probably think I have made it all up; but I can assure you it is true. At my age it is not necessary to tell lies. And although the incident occurred at a time when my state of mind could be described as fragile, I have no difficulty in recalling every detail of that strange morning last summer.

I was in Oslo, and was nearing the end of a stay at the Hotel Continental. I remember that I had overslept that morning, and when I arrived in the small breakfast room there was only one other guest still eating – a tall, white-haired gentleman with whom I had exchanged polite good mornings since my arrival a few days before.

I helped myself to some fruit juice and a small bread roll and chose a seat by the window, close enough to my fellow guest so as to appear companionable if he wished to strike up a conversation, but far enough away to allow him the opportunity to enjoy his breakfast in silence. I do not mind eating alone, but I find that other solitary diners often feel the need to invite themselves to join you, to join forces so that you both seem less conspicuous. I like the company of handsome men, and this one was singularly attractive and very well dressed. And if I had read the signals correctly – I consider myself something of an expert when it comes to body language – my fellow diner would welcome an opportunity to introduce himself.

As I sat down the man looked up from his plate and gave me a warm smile, which I returned, wished me good morning then went back to his coffee and newspaper. I noticed, as I ate, that he was giving me long appraising looks over the top of his paper, but whenever I inadvertently caught his eye he just smiled again and returned to his reading. I thought that perhaps he was shy, and wondered whether I myself should make the first move to strike up a conversation.

I have said that my state of mind was rather fragile at the time, and I feel I ought to explain why this was so, because although it has no bearing on what happened that morning, it does perhaps explain my own immediate reaction to the incident. I had been jilted, you see. Silly, isn't it, for a woman of sixty-five to be jilted. But it does happen. It was to be my third marriage; my first ended in divorce, the second with my husband's death. Henry had come into my life during the early months of my widowhood and lifted me from my melancholy. We had planned to marry when a suitable period of mourning had been observed, a year we had decided, and had made all the arrangements, sent invitations, booked a honeymoon. Then two days before the wedding he sent me a letter saying that he had met someone else.

When I had spent my fury and dried my tears, I did what I have always done in times of stress. I ran away. I have run away to various locations over the years – New York, Madrid, Paris, Lisbon – and have never regretted it. It makes me feel adventurous, independent, and I always return strengthened and renewed. Never with my tail between my legs. I had visited Oslo many times with my late husband. Perhaps, at that time, I wanted to feel close to him once more.

I had just finished my second cup of coffee and was looking out of the window across the street at a group of tourists standing in front of the National Theatre, whose guide was explaining to them either the history or the architectural merits of the building, when suddenly a young girl came running out of the Metro, pushed her way through the crowd towards the statue of the actor, Per Aabel, at the side of the theatre, hauled herself up onto its plinth, and stood with her arms tightly clasped around its shiny head.

Intrigued by this unexpected sight I stood up and moved closer to the window to get a better view. My fellow diner, sensing that something untoward had happened outside, also left his table and came to stand beside me, close beside me as it happens, because there was very little space between the table and the window. I explained to him what I had seen, and as we stood watching the unfolding drama I enjoyed the feel of his jacket brushing against my bare arm, the smell of his cologne, his nearness.

We saw a young man approaching the statue and a shouted conversation ensued, he gesticulating wildly, she with angry movements of the head. I leant forward and opened the window in order to hear better, although I spoke no Norwegian. My companion also leant forward, pressing even closer, and began to translate what was happening.

"He is afraid she might fall and hurt herself. He says he does not know why she is behaving this way. She is angry because she saw him with another woman last night. It is nothing, he says, he can explain all that. There is no need for explanations. She has found out that he is a paid escort. He says it is good money, there is no sex involved. She says he should find a decent job, even if it pays less. He says he needs the money because he wants to marry her now and not wait until they have both finished university. Can she believe him? Why should she? Because I love you very much, he says."

At this point I could see the change of expression on the girl's face. She slid down the bronze Per Aabel's back and leaned towards the man, who lifted her down from the statue and held her in a passionate embrace. The onlookers tactfully began to disperse as the young couple, oblivious, stood holding each other tightly, lips locked together, almost motionless.

As I came away from the window, happy but slightly embarrassed at what I had witnessed, I turned into the arms of the handsome white-haired man who looked straight into my eyes, pulled me gently towards him, and gave me a long lingering kiss, which I unhesitatingly returned. Then he stepped back, smiled, and walked quickly out of the dining room.

I never saw him again.

Alice Goes Shopping

It was only a very small collision. Just a bump really, but the sound of splintering glass made heads turn. With the handle of her trolley Alice had just caught the edge of one of the special Christmas displays at the corner of an aisle – champagne glasses, in boxes of six, free with two bottles of the supermarket's own brand of Cava.

None of the boxes had fallen, although some had been knocked askew, but the half dozen samples exhibited on top of the pyramid so that shoppers could appreciate the quality of the generous offer, were now on the floor. Only one had smashed.

A young girl wearing flashing snowman earrings, who had been stocking the shelves opposite, called for a brush and shovel as some of the shoppers rushed to help.

"If they'd been crystal they'd all have shattered," someone said. They all laughed, and another voice commented:

"Stupid place to put a display anyway."

It was a minor blip at the start of a busy morning. No big deal. A diversion that would soon be forgotten. So they were all surprised to see Alice burst into tears.

"Oh, I'm so sorry… so sorry," wept Alice.

One of the shoppers came over to comfort her.

"Now don't upset yourself. It was an accident. These trolleys seem to have a will of their own sometimes." She put her arm round Alice's shoulder. The others who had stopped to stare or help now moved off, slightly embarrassed.

The young assistant, whose name badge said "Cheryl", bent down to sweep up the glass, and smiling up at Alice asked her name.

"Alice," she sobbed. "Alice Price. I'm so sorry. Really, I can't believe I could have been so careless." She wept into her handkerchief.

"Well, Alice, you shouldn't upset yourself. There's only one glass broken. You should see some of the stuff that gets smashed in here every day. Bottles of wine, jars of jam, eggs…"

The woman with her arm round Alice raised her eyebrows at Cheryl, to suggest that she might want to shut up. She had noticed that Alice wasn't just holding tightly to her trolley, she was being supported by it. She looked as if she was on the point of collapse.

"Look, couldn't she sit down somewhere? Maybe your staff room? She might like a nice cup of tea."

"Don't see why not," said the girl brightly. Then remembering that she was merely a junior member of staff added quietly: "I'd better just ask the manager first."

Alice wobbled slightly, and gave the woman, who introduced herself as Myra, a weak smile. The way Myra seemed to take charge made Alice wonder if she was a schoolteacher; she seemed to have an air of authority about her. Or perhaps she was a policewoman. She was certainly very tall.

"You're very kind. I just don't know what's wrong with me lately, I've become so clumsy, always bumping into things. I never used to be like this. Not when Harry was alive. I looked after him so well. We were so happy together, didn't need anyone else. Not even children. But now he's gone I just don't seem to be able to get things together. It's a terrible curse old age. Especially when you're on your own." The tears started to flow again, silently this time.

Poor old soul's probably depressed, thought Myra. But as she looked closely at Alice she wondered. She didn't look very old, early seventies probably, though it was often hard to tell. She was smartly dressed, hair neatly done, and she'd put on a bit of lipstick and powder that morning.

Alice seemed to read her thoughts.

"I try so hard," she wept. "But I live in a block of flats, and the neighbours are all couples or young families. Nobody wants to be bothered with an old woman. I know they all have their own lives to get on with. I understand that, it's only natural. It's just that I get so tearful nowadays. Really, I don't know what's wrong with me."

Myra knew exactly what was wrong and it could be summed up in one word. Loneliness. Her heart went out to Alice. She knew very well that her own mother might have been in the same situation when her father had died if Myra hadn't persuaded her to go into sheltered housing. Now she had some very good friends around her and an active social life. Best of all, her new set-up meant she could choose when she wanted company and when she wanted to be alone. What a pity Alice didn't have a family to help her. Maybe she should have a social worker…

Alice saw Cheryl walking towards them and behind her a rather chubby man in a jacket and tie. The manager, probably. He looked kind and friendly. Alice dried her tears. She didn't want them all to think she was one of those people who whined and complained all day. That was no way to behave. No, she had a lot to be thankful for. And now they were going to have a nice cup of tea and a chat. Myra would probably come along to keep her company, and maybe Cheryl would be allowed to stay too. She smiled at them all. Such pleasant people.

It was almost lunch time when Alice stepped out of the lift and rummaged in her handbag for her key.

Home to an empty house, she thought sadly as she opened the door. But it didn't matter. She'd had a lovely morning and made some new friends. Cheryl was a delightful young girl, such a cheerful personality, full of fun. You would never be bored with Cheryl around. And Mr Wilson – who said she could call him Bob, but she felt that was inappropriate. He was the manager after all, even if it wasn't one of the more well-known supermarkets. He had given her a small box of chocolates as she left the store. So kind.

Not as kind as the manager of Asda at the other end of town though. He had given her a huge bunch of flowers and a fruit cake, and a cup of tea and a bun in their café. And she'd made much more of a mess in his shop. She hadn't expected the bags of sugar to burst as they fell because they weren't piled very high. She didn't like the thought of all that waste, so she was more careful after that. Tins were okay though, and so were non food items. Like those glasses today.

She thought again of Mr Wilson and young Cheryl. She'd have to remember to send them a Christmas card. And Myra, of course. The schoolteacher, as she had rightly guessed. A head teacher actually. How sweet of Myra to invite her for dinner on Christmas day. She would meet Myra's husband, and her mother would be there too.

"It won't be any trouble to set one more place at the table," she had assured Alice.

How kind. She must take Myra a nice present. Perhaps that big tin of biscuits with the nice picture on it that they'd given her in Sainsbury's last Sunday. When she had knocked over the pile of newspapers and magazines just inside the door.

So many presents, Alice thought happily as she placed the small box of chocolates under her Christmas tree beside the other parcels. She didn't usually have such a large tree, but Mrs Evans had insisted. She was one of the managers in Marks & Spencer's. She'd sent her two sons round to decorate it. Everyone was so kind to an old lady, Alice thought.

It was such fun making new friends.

Therapy

Iris had hoped to start her crossword as she sat in the waiting room, but Andrew arrived just behind her so she didn't bother taking the newspaper out of her bag. She didn't want to be rude; Andrew was always cheery, and he liked to chat. He liked reading, so they often discussed books.

"What's it today then?" he asked as he sat down beside her.

"Sore knee. It's been sore for six months. It's a problem going up stairs and I'm taking a lot of Paracetamol, but it's not helping much. I'm getting depressed."

Andrew nodded.

"I've got a bad tummy bug. It's lasted two weeks and I've been taking Imodium. I'm not long back from a holiday in North West China."

"Oh, I love doing that one," said Iris, laughing. "Their faces when you say you work on the deli counter at Tesco."

"My favourite's the bad back. I always exaggerate the number of painkillers I'm taking, and I tell them I smoke four joints a day for relief. They know that's not in the script and you can see some of them trying not to laugh."

"You're incorrigible, Andrew. We're supposed to be helping them to develop good communication skills, not trying to entertain them."

"The rules don't state that a Volunteer Patient must keep a straight face at all times, do they?"

Iris was called in to the doctor's room before she could reply. The young student looked, as indeed he was, fresh out of school. He had the speech for his imaginary situation well rehearsed.

"I'm Paul Monaghan and I'm a medical student," he said in a strong Irish accent, as he shook her hand. "The doctor has asked me to speak to you before you go in to see him, as part of my training, is that okay with you?" He didn't wait for an answer. "Can I just check your name? Jean Smith, isn't it? And what's your date of birth?"

Iris was surprised at his confidence; most of them were very nervous the first time, especially since they were being evaluated by fellow students who were always happy to point out mistakes and omissions. She wondered what Andrew would have made of this boy.

"The 5th of January 1970."

She watched to see if he would express surprise, but he wasn't listening properly. That date would have put her in her forties. A snort at the back of the room suggested one of his peer group had done the maths.

"And what have you come to see the doctor about today?" The young man leaned forward and made eye contact. That would be a tick for Good Body Language.

Iris stared into his warm brown eyes and confessed:

"I'm a bit depressed. Well, more than a bit. I'm really, really depressed."

Over in the corner she saw the tutor look up sharply from his notes, then riffle through them, no doubt confused because this wasn't the scenario he had in front of him. The student frowned, but continued regardless:

"And how long have you felt like this?"

"Since my husband died." She hadn't meant to say that. She had meant to revert to the original script, but somehow… it just came out.

"Oh dear," young Monaghan carried on gamely. He leaned over and patted her hand. "You must miss him very much."

She felt her throat constricting, her eyes threatening tears. She hadn't expected this boy to be kind.

"Yes, I do. And… you see… he was cremated... I brought home his ashes…and..."

Iris wasn't sure what she was trying to say. She could see the tutor becoming agitated. The student, nodding like a car ornament, seemed lost for words and was perhaps beginning to panic; then, remembering his notes, he interrupted a pause:

"Do you mind if I ask you a few questions about your lifestyle?" He didn't wait for a reply. "Do you smoke?"

The abrupt change of tack brought Iris back into the moment.

"No."

"Do you drink alcohol?"

Iris let the student know she was thinking hard about the question.

"Yes."

"How many units of alcohol would you say you drink each day?"

"I don't know anything about units. I have a couple of glasses of wine with my dinner every night. Red wine, I hear it's good for you. And I have a G and T or two before I go to bed."

Before the boy could reckon this up, she added:

"It helps me sleep at night. I have problems getting off. Because of my sore knee."

She could feel the room relaxing. Paul Monaghan smiled and leaned towards her again, relieved to be back on course.

"And how long has the knee been bothering you?"

Five minutes later Iris was back in the waiting area with Andrew.

How's the sore knee?" he asked.

"It's in danger of turning me into an alcoholic," she said. "How's your diarrhoea?"

"Getting worse by the minute. I've developed severe stomach cramps. I think I'll change the holiday destination to Kazakhstan, for variation."

"Why do we do this, Andrew?"

"Lots of reasons. To help the next generation of doctors. To save the medical school having to pay for proper actors. To keep our memories active. To get a free lunch at the canteen. No, strike that one out. The food here's terrible."

They both laughed.

"I read an interesting story last night," said Iris. "It was about a woman whose husband had died and she was trying to fill her days. She did a lot of voluntary work."

She could feel the barrier go up at the mention of death.

"Doesn't sound like something I'd want to read. I don't like fiction. I prefer real life."

Iris continued as if she hadn't heard him.

"I think the message the author was trying to get across was that people who volunteer don't usually do it for altruistic reasons. They do it because they like having someone to talk to. It's a kind of therapy."

"Absolute tosh!"

"That's what I thought at first, but then… well…you know… it's good to talk."

Andrew guffawed.

"You sound like that old BT advert."

Iris laughed too.

They sat in companionable silence for a while, until Andrew said:

"I do it to get out of the house."

"Yes," said Iris. "There's that too."

Andrew leaned over and asked, quietly:

"Have you decided what to do with the ashes yet?"

Iris shook her head.

She had told Andrew a few weeks ago about the problem of her husband's ashes. She couldn't decide whether Bill would like to be scattered on the golf course, where he'd spent half of his spare time, or down at the river, where he'd spent the other half, fishing. Or somewhere else entirely. Meanwhile he'd been in a casket on a shelf in the kitchen for almost a year, waiting. Maybe he was quite happy there.

"He probably wouldn't care where his ashes were put, as long as they're with yours – eventually."

"Thank you, Andrew. I hadn't considered that."

She had considered it; but where would that be? She didn't fancy the golf course or the river. She'd have to find somewhere they would both be happy – or at least rest in peace. Well, there was no rush. She would keep him close a while yet.

They sat in silence again until a door opened and a young girl tiptoed out, looking towards them nervously. When she spoke it was almost a whisper:

"Emm… Mrs Smith?"

"Not me," said Andrew brightly.

Iris stood up and beamed a smile at the student, hoping to convey her willingness to help the girl through this ordeal. She would try to behave herself this time.

Neighbours

(A very short story)

Maureen died a couple of weeks ago. They took her out in a yellow coffin – the undertakers. No sign of any mourners though, even though she always had a lot of visitors. Well-dressed city types mostly. She was well-dressed too, in her own way. If you like black leather.

The Council gave her flat to a homeless man – Eddie. I met him on the stairs the day he moved in and he invited me up to look around.

The sitting room was all black and had whips and chains hanging on the wall. The bedroom was done up with bricks and bars like a police cell. There was a bed in the bathroom instead of a bath, and everything was white, like a hospital.

She was a dominatrix, Eddie said. I didn't know what that was but I went to the library and looked it up. Oh well. Takes all sorts doesn't it?

I miss Maureen. She was a bit noisy, but I didn't mind that – the banging and scraping, and counting. She was always counting out loud. That Eddie's very quiet. Too quiet. I think he's up to something up there.